"Do not be afraid," he whispered to her

Cally wanted to tell him she wasn't afraid but was so unsure what she felt, she didn't say anything. And at the moment his upward-moving hands touched her breasts, his lips claimed hers and she clutched at him again, breathing his name, "Javier!"

The urgency growing in her had her wanting more, yet more. To feel his hardness against her, that same raging need, had her heart hammering, as hoarsely he murmured, *"Te quiero,"* pressing himself to her.

"What...does that mean?" she whispered, only then beginning to feel any sort of nervousness.

Tenderly Javier smiled down at her. "I want you," he translated. And, on a breath, *"Te amo."*

JESSICA STEELE
is also the author of these
Harlequin Romances

These books may be available at your local bookseller.

For a free catalog listing all titles currently available,
send your name and address to:

HARLEQUIN READER SERVICE
1440 South Priest Drive, Tempe, AZ 85281
Canadian address: Stratford, Ontario N5A 6W2

Tethered Liberty

Jessica Steele

Harlequin Books

TORONTO • NEW YORK • LONDON
AMSTERDAM • PARIS • SYDNEY • HAMBURG
STOCKHOLM • ATHENS • TOKYO • MILAN

Original hardcover edition published in 1983
by Mills & Boon Limited

ISBN 0-373-02580-7

Harlequin Romance first edition October 1983

Printed in U.S.A.

CHAPTER ONE

SHE had over two hours to wait. Cally Shearman had never been away from home before. She was unaccustomed to the feeling of excitement that had begun generating in her from that initial moment of leaving behind just toying with the idea, and of staying with that notion that touched down—why shouldn't she?

Of course, there had been one very big fly in the ointment: her father. Bernard Shearman had ruled her and her brother Rolfe with a stern rod of iron, and even though she was now twenty-three she had thought she would never escape.

Perhaps there had been something basically lacking in her from the start, she mused. Though since she, unlike Rolfe, had never been allowed to go to university, to get out and mix with other people her own age, when Rolfe had suggested two years ago that she 'leave the old man to his own devices and come with me'; though wanting to share the same excitement that had been in his eyes, she just hadn't been able to do it.

She didn't know whether it was because she had any affection for her father that she had stayed, or if it was from duty only that she had told Rolfe, 'He needs me.' Who else would fetch and carry for him if she left? He was a vain man, her father, and idle. He was used to having his shoes polished for him, his linen immaculate, and demanded three cooked meals a day, though he seemed helpless to so much as boil an egg for himself.

A paroxysm of coughing took her, causing the kindly

transatlantic lady sitting next to her to enquire, 'Are
you all right, dear?'

Cally wiped moisture engendered by the coughing
attack from her eyes. 'Perfectly, thank you,' she
replied sedately, sitting up straight in the wide purple
and white armchair in the transit lounge of Miami
airport.

The woman gave her a look that filed her away as
some stuffy English female, letting her know her
reserved manner had offended. And, spontaneity of any
sort sternly repressed from as far back as she could
remember, Cally just couldn't find the words to tell the
woman how much she appreciated her kind enquiry.

Embarrassed at her own ineptitude, she opened her
bag and took out the letter she already knew by heart.
The letter that had come from Rolfe in Mexico two
months ago. It had arrived at the same time as things
had begun to change at home.

She made a pretence of being immersed in the letter
in her hand, recalling that she had been ill at the time,
victim to some strong 'flu virus that much to the
annoyance of her father had kept her in bed two days.

But if that neglected virus had knocked her normally
healthy body sideways, had left her listless and tired,
and with a cough that attacked and didn't help to make
her feel any better, she had grown of the opinion that it
was worth all of it. For her father, not demeaning
himself to kitchen chores—which made it just as well
her appetite had been affected—had opted to eat out.
In the course of doing so, he had met and made friends
with a widow, Elma Bates. She was about five years his
junior, and for all she appeared as bossy as him, he had
got on with her like a house on fire.

Cally remembered that first day he had brought Mrs
Bates home. 'Don't slouch,' he had sharply rebuked her
when, still feeling ghastly, she knew her usually straight

shoulders were rounded as she carried a tea tray in from the kitchen.

'You've had a cold, your father tells me,' Elma Bates had remarked, her thin lips parting in a straight line, the best she could manage in the way of a smile.

'I'm better now,' she had replied—and had promptly, and unforgivably in her father's eyes, broken out into a fit of coughing, slopping tea into the saucer of the cup she was just about to hand to Mrs Bates.

'Are you taking anything for that cough?' Elma Bates enquired, backing away, though whether she was afraid of germs or a tea rinse, Cally was undecided.

'The doctor says her cough will clear as soon as we have some sunshine,' her father had answered for her, and his eyes went to the window where rain was pouring down. 'Look at it—May, and not a sign of summer!'

Elma Bates favoured him with a look as though he had said something brilliantly witty, and, tea served, Cally sat down, her thoughts drifting to Rolfe, to the letter she had received from him that morning, and to the sunshine he must be experiencing in abundance. It was kind of him to invite her to his wedding, but she didn't stand an earthly chance of going. Rolfe by the sound of it had really landed on his feet. He must have a good job out there in Querétaro, she mused, to be able to invite her to stay as long as she liked. 'Money no object,' he had written. 'Just pack your bags and come. I've got a big house waiting for Graciela and me to move into—we could go for days without seeing you.'

Cally smiled at her thoughts. It would be nice to go and see her only brother married. And if she stayed with them—he and Graciela newly wed as they would be—she would certainly make herself scarce. But of course she wouldn't be going. Even if Rolfe had said, knowing their money situation, that all she needed to do was to scrape up the fare one way; that he would pay her return flight if and when she wanted to return home.

'May we share the joke?'

Her father's acid remark brought her attention back into the room. 'I'm sorry, Father,' she said obediently. 'I was—er—just thinking about Rolfe.'

'He's about to be married, I believe,' inserted Elma Bates. And with an arch look at Bernard Shearman, 'You don't look old enough to have a son about to be married.'

Nausea hit Cally. Rolfe was twenty-eight! Admitted, her father was a dapper man, and did look younger than his years, but he was sixty, for goodness' sake, had taken early retirement, and had been glad to do so.

As soon as she could, she politely left them to it and escaped to the kitchen, where, slumped on to a chair, she wished she could find some energy from somewhere. Apart from the rare occasion when an aunt or uncle on her dead mother's side would drop in and be served the obligatory cup of tea, her father never entertained, but since Mrs Bates didn't look like making a move, Cally was set to wondering if she would be invited to stay to dinner.

In the weeks that followed, Elma Bates became a frequent visitor to the house. And if a change was to be seen in Bernard Shearman in that he appeared to be more mellow after each of the widow's visits, then a change was happening in Cally too. Though she was still experiencing bouts of listlessness, some of her former energy returned. She thought often of Rolfe, whose reaction to their strict upbringing, in contrast to her own, had been for him to go rather wild once he'd got to university. He must have settled down now he had fallen in love with Graciela Delgadillo, she thought, and felt good inside for him, though she was aware she could never be like him—although she wished that she could.

But to be careless whether she had a job or not, to flout convention the way he had often done, so much so that her father had refused to allow him back in the house after his studies were completed, was not her way. Her father had done a good job in repressing her natural instincts, she thought. But in admitting that, it was then that a rebellion she didn't know she had in her soul started to stir.

She began to welcome the sour Elma Bates' visits. Began to hope that if he was not in love with the woman, her view of her father being that he was incapable of loving, then he would see her as a more fitting companion to end his days with than herself who had never had the courage to face his wrath and tell him she was leaving.

It was two weeks before Rolfe was due to be married, when she was busy in the kitchen, while this time her father was visiting Elma Bates' home, that the growing rebellion inside her surged up and just wouldn't stay down. She heard her father's key in the door, but instead of that something that stirred in her disappearing on knowing he was near, this time it stayed. Stayed, making it impossible for her to hang around waiting and waiting for something to develop between him and his lady-friend.

Bernard Shearman came into the kitchen, a thing he seldom did, his only interest being in what came out of it; there was no desire in him to see how each culinary effort came into being. That he appeared disposed to linger was something new, and Cally found then that she wasn't waiting if he had come into her domain to criticise, and was getting in there first with what was in her mind.

Not looking at him, she stirred the soup they were to have that night, and began while her nerve lasted, 'I've been thinking——' and overwhelmingly aware from the stillness, that he was listening, she swallowed, and said, 'I've been thinking that—that I'd like to go and see Rolfe married.'

The loudspeaker in the transit lounge, broadcasting for someone, brought her back to her surroundings. Cally gazed at Rolfe's letter still in her hand, and wondered if he had received her letter. He must have done, she thought. His letters took about nine days to reach her, and she had written to him the very next day.

A gentle smile played round her beautiful mouth as she imagined his surprise at what she had written, that not only would she be there to see him married tomorrow; but at the rest of her news.

She had had to look at her father after she had dared to tell him what *she* wanted to do for a change, and had seen, as she had expected, that he looked angry. But that anger, she realised later, had only been because she had upstaged him. He had news of his own that he had been about to impart, and he hadn't liked it that his browbeaten daughter was suddenly showing that she had more nerve than he had given her credit for.

Her statement of what she would like to do had for the moment been ignored. 'Mrs Bates is coming to dinner—she's to be your new mother—make sure you've got enough for three.' With that announcement, leaving Cally standing open-mouthed, he had stomped tetchily out of the kitchen.

But having not grown any fonder of Elma Bates, Cally had that evening found reason to be grateful to her. It was obvious, when they were all seated round the dinner table, that her father had discussed her wish to go to Mexico with his future bride. For in the solemn atmosphere of the meal, her hopes of going to Mexico were dim since he had chosen to ignore her stated desire, and since she didn't have the wherewithal for her ticket, Cally put her disappointment behind her and forced a pleasant smile.

'I didn't get to congratulate you, Father,' she said quietly, and turning to Elma Bates, 'I'm very pleased, Mrs Bates. I'm sure you'll . . .'

Mrs Bates shrugged away her congratulations. 'Bernard tells me you want to go to your brother's wedding in two weeks' time.'

Taken aback, Cally swung her grey-green eyes on to her father. He was continuing with his meal, perfectly content to leave all the talking to Mrs Bates, apparently.

'Yes—that's right,' she replied quietly. 'He's my only brother and . . .'

'We think you should go,' announced Mrs Bates as though it had all been settled. And Cally's delight was such that it just wouldn't be squashed that the thin-lipped woman clearly didn't care for her either, as she went on to say, 'Bernard will be selling this house and moving in with me.' And looking straight at her, not a blink about her, 'My home isn't big enough for the three of us.'

And I'm glad about that, Cally thought, up in her room later, appreciating just how lucky she was in escaping the possible fate of being skivvy to both her father and his new wife.

But she was to learn the next day that if Mrs Bates had managed to mellow her father a little, then he was none the more generous with his money than he had ever been, even if he could anticipate doing very nicely from the sale of the house.

'I'll pay for your ticket—one way,' he informed her.

'But . . .' she began, then saw just how uncaring her parent was about her. 'You're saying you don't want me to come back?' It was the first time she had ever challenged him, and to her surprise she discovered she should have done it years ago—he had a coward's streak in him.

'I didn't say that,' he blustered. 'Your brother said he'd pay your return fare, didn't he? He's got more money than me—let him pay!'

Cally didn't like it. But since she hadn't yet got as far as having the money in her hands for even a one-way ticket, she didn't dare push it; her father had been known to go back on his word before.

'Is there a chance I could have a little extra to buy a couple of dresses? It's bound to be very hot out there.' His reply was lost as a bout of coughing took her. Though she was sure it was not because she had aroused his sympathy that he gave her a cheque to cover her air fare with enough for a couple of dresses and a small amount of pocket money left over.

One of the friendly ground staff came and grouped the dozen or so people who were continuing on to Mexico City together. Cally stood up, and knew excitement again as she trooped with the others to the waiting plane. Would Rolfe be meeting her at Mexico City? She couldn't wait to see him.

The flight from Miami was fairly smooth. The DC10, more congenial than the jumbo that had brought her the first leg, she thought, took two hours and forty minutes before it touched down on Mexican soil. And any tiredness she was feeling was evaporated by the thought that once through Customs, she might be seeing the brother she loved so dearly.

He *must* have got my letter, she thought, standing to look again and again, trying to see Rolfe. Disappointment hit her that he wasn't there to meet her, but she swallowed it down. Querétaro was about a hundred and twenty miles away from the capital, after all. And with the wedding arranged for tomorrow, he probably had masses to do. He might even have a stag night planned, she mused, tiredness coming over her, because although it was only half past six in the afternoon Mexico time, it was half past one tomorrow morning back in England.

Well, she wasn't getting to Querétaro by standing here looking like some lost soul, was she? Remembering that in one of his few letters Rolfe had said there was a regular coach service to Querétaro, armed with her Mexican phrase book and her two suitcases, Cally went in search of a taxi to take her to the coach station.

Tiredness that excitement at seeing Rolfe had kept at bay tugged at her eyelids, though in the blare of car horns and furious driving on the way to the coach station, any sleep would not have been longer than the forty seconds variety.

Her phrase book came in more than useful when she had been deposited at the coach station and purchased a ticket. She was directed to a bus which, although it said 'Leon', she was assured would take her to Querétaro. Finding a seat, she breathed a sigh of relief mixed with not a little pleasure—she had made it this far!

'Perdón, señorita,' said the stockily built Mexican who came and sat next to her as one of the two small children he gathered on his lap knocked into her.

She had seen him in conversation with a woman with two other children he had just seated on the other side of the aisle, and guessed she was his wife. And suddenly Cally was smiling, a natural smile that went further than merely acknowledging the Mexican's apology. Repressed spontaneity was all at once having a battle for release, was refusing to be imprisoned any longer. And before she knew it she was offering, by gestures, to change places so husband and wife could sit together. She even risked a 'De nada'—you are welcome—in answer to his, 'Muchas gracias,' as the family of six sat together. And seeing the wealth of love in the man for

his children in the way he handled them, love she and
Rolfe had never known from their father, she knew
right then that she was just going to love Mexico.

By the time the coach reached Querétaro, Cally was
near to being out on her feet. The bus journey had
taken three hours, and it was now dark. But she had
been afraid to close her eyes in case she was asleep and
went past her destination.

Her cases were handed to her from the side luggage
compartment of the coach, and as she made her way
wearily inside the coach station, it took all the reserve
from her upbringing for her not to break down in tears
that there was no Rolfe there in Querétaro to meet her.

'You look lost,' said a chirpy English voice, and she
was fighting tears again as she saw the youth with his
girl-companion, student types she thought, with their
jeans and haversacks. 'We've an age to wait for our
transport, need any help?'

Feeling less alone just to hear the friendly English
couple, Cally explained that she had hoped to have her
brother there to meet her, and excusing Rolfe,
explained about him being married tomorrow. 'He must
be terribly busy,' she ended.

'Or having a rave-up somewhere on his last night of
freedom,' grinned the young man, earning a dig in the
ribs from his girl-friend. 'Still, you'll know where he
lives.'

Cally took the letter from her bag showing the
address of Rolfe's flat. Whereupon the young man
advised her that it wasn't very far, they themselves were
as near broke as made no difference, but if she was up
to a taxi they would go with her and explain to the
landlord, since they spoke the lingo, who she was and
get him to let her into Rolfe's flat, should he, as the
young man suspected, be out on the town somewhere.

Whether they could see how weary she was—it must be

getting on for five in the morning in England, she calculated—she didn't know. But they each relieved her of a case, and were soon hailing a taxi.

Disappointment awaited her at the address the taxi took them to, for on rousing the landlord, who fortunately lived on the premises, and no Rolfe answering the ring at his door, they discovered he had that morning vacated his flat.

'He must have moved his things into his house ready for when he and Graciela return from their honeymoon,' she said, trying not to look as despondent as she felt— or to feel such a fool either when Tim, as she discovered his name was, asked the address of her brother's house, in having to tell him she didn't know because Rolfe hadn't thought to tell her.

She then thought her mentioning the name Graciela must have triggered some idea in the landlord, for with a babble of Spanish he was addressing Tim, the only words she being able to isolate being *'novia'* which she knew meant fiancée, and 'Señor Delgadillo' the name Delgadillo being familiar. But the smile on Tim's face as he offered his, *'Gracias, señor,'* to the landlord showed that he, at any rate, didn't think not knowing where Rolfe now lived was too much of a problem.

'Apparently your brother is engaged to a daughter of one of the most respected men in the city,' Tim told her. 'Señor Delgadillo has a large engineering works in the area, and just everybody knows where he lives—a very up-market area.' He trotted out the address the landlord had given him.

'You think I should go there?' Cally asked uncertainly, though she couldn't see what else she could do.

'Nothing else for it,' said Tim. 'There's a very good chance your brother will be there, I'd say. And if he isn't, then they'll soon be able to tell you where his new abode is.'

Her heart was already lifting. Just the thought that Rolfe could very well be at his fiancée's home was enough to have her spirits rising.

The young couple carried her cases as they walked to a main street to find a taxi, Tim telling her on the way that they wouldn't have time to go with her, and Cally giving them both her heartfelt thanks, of the opinion they had done more than enough for her already. And though she didn't have too much money to spare herself, she wished they would have accepted her offer of their own taxi fare back to the coach station.

'We'll hoof it,' said Tim, and with a disarming grin, 'It'll do Julie good, she's put on weight since we've been here.'

'Compliments yet,' said Julie, but grinned back, in no way put out.

Cally was sorry to part from the two friendly people. Slow to make friends, she was surprised at how easily she had got along with them. And she paused to wonder, as the taxi sped under a giant high and many-arched aqueduct, whether it was because she was away from her father that that introvert streak in her was fading.

After a taxi journey that seemed to go on for ever, the driver turned into a cobblestoned area lined with trees. It was well lit and smart, and fully up to Tim's 'up-market' terminology. Having not a clue about the fare—Tim had extracted some notes from her small supply of Mexican currency before—she trusted her luck and handed the taxi driver a five-hundred-peso note, worth somewhere in the region of ten pounds, she thought, and discovered it was more than enough when the driver handed her some change.

She felt alone and not a little nervous as the taxi drove away at speed. The avenue was so quiet, high walls surrounded the house, and double doors about twelve feet high confronted her, giving her the impression that no one would hear when she pressed the bell.

She pressed again when no one answered her first ring. Supposing the Delgadillo family were out too? Panic rose in her. She knew she just wouldn't have the nerve to go ringing on anyone else's door if no one answered this one.

Suddenly she heard a dog barking, then footsteps. Then she was concentrating on the little Spanish she knew, though she was hopeful the person she could hear pulling back bolts knew a little English.

'Perdon,' she said, when at last an opening appeared in the woodwork, though the girl there was giving her only half her attention as she hung on to the red setter who was still furiously barking and trying his best to get out through the opening. 'Er—Señor Shearman *en casa*?'

Her attempt was greeted by a blank look from the girl. And then to her bewilderment, she promptly closed the door on her.

What . . .? Cally got as far as thinking as she stood there with her mouth agape. She then realised the girl must have gone to shut the troublesome dog in. She had probably only brought it with her in the first place in case it was some unsavoury character who had rung the bell, she thought. That realisation was followed by a far happier thought as she heard firm masculine footsteps near the stout doors; the girl must have understood her, must have gone away to fetch Rolfe.

Tiredness vanished instantly at the thought. Her mouth began to curve as she straightened up, pushing her long blonde hair back from her face. The footsteps had halted, the door was being opened. Her smile broadened and she went to take a step forward, she was

ready for the bear-hug Rolfe would give her, was ready
to see the pleased astonishment on his face.

Then abruptly her smile faded. For the man who
stood there was not Rolfe. He was a man about five or
ten years older than her brother, tall like him, with
broad shoulders like him. But he was looking so
nowhere near being pleased to see her standing there
outlined in the street lamp that Cally went cold all over.

He was a man who had no time to waste either, she
soon heard. For either deducing from her blonde hair
that she was not Mexican, or gathering from what the
girl must have told him that it was a foreigner at the
door, he addressed her straight away in her own tongue.

'The maid tells me you are asking for Shearman,' he
said grittily, no welcome there in a voice which bore
little trace of an accent.

'Yes,' she said quietly, taking an instant dislike to
him, her voice as cold as his, as she wished it had been
possible for Julie and Tim, her own friendly country-
men, to have come with her. 'I'm . . .' she began, her
voice no warmer, something in this man bringing back
to life the introvert in her she had been on the way to
saying goodbye to.

'You're another of his women,' the man cut her off.

'*What?*'

Shock was taking her at what he said. Something was
wrong! It had to be if he was Señor Delgadillo—though
he had to have married very young to be Graciela's
father—yet he was talking of Rolfe and other women!

'My name is Cally Shearman,' she told him icily. She
loved her brother, nobody was going to cast aspersions
on him and get her being any warmer. 'Rolfe is my
brother. I have just arrived from England. I have come
for his wedding tomorrow.'

For ageless moments the man studied her, but she
was determined in the face of his hostility that he

shouldn't, as tiredness grabbed at her again, see her wilt. Stiffly she held herself erect under his scrutiny. She was uncaring what he made of her reed-like slimness, her every feature exposed to his view as from her blonde hair and clear pale skin his eyes travelled from her smooth forehead, to her dainty, tending-to-be-aristocratic nose, to linger on her shapely mouth, to her chin, which only now she realised was right to have that suggestion of stubbornness about it. For although she wanted to run away and hide from his narrow-eyed gaze, she was equally determined that she wasn't moving a step until she knew what was wrong, what it was this Señor Delgadillo, if he was Graciela's father, had against Rolfe, with his talk of 'You're another of his women.'

The man finished his inspection of her by finally flicking his gaze down over her figure, then at last he spoke, his voice no more welcoming, when he said harshly:

'You had better come in.'

'Rolfe is here?'

Cally could have saved her breath. She was ignored as effortlessly her cases were hefted through the opening in the massive doors, and dumped inside. Still without answering, the man stood back to allow her through the opening. And it was then, while waiting as he closed and bolted the door, that Cally began to more than dislike him, as meekly she was made to follow as he led the way along a terrace and into a well-illuminated living room.

A perfunctory wave of his hand indicated that he wanted her to sit before he himself sat down. Cally sat, mainly because she was used to being told what to do, but also because now she was able to see the man more clearly as she looked up into the bluest of eyes, her new-found obstinacy was taken over by the surprise she felt

that, for all that trace of accent, he didn't look her idea
of a Mexican at all.

It annoyed her too, as her eyes registered that his hair
was nearly as fair as Rolfe's dark blond, that he was still
standing, had her at a disadvantage in that he had never
intended to be seated anyway. And as for aristocratic
noses, his had all the aristocracy one could wish for, as
unspeaking he looked down the straightness of it at her.

The arrogant way he was looking at her stirred that
in her that said for too long she had been confined by
the strictures of her upbringing. She hadn't come all
this way to have it follow her, to have it continue. And
there was hauteur in her voice as she demanded to
know:

'Are you Señor Delgadillo?'

'Carlos Delgadillo is my cousin,' she was informed,
the ice in those blue eyes telling her he wasn't liking her
manner. And before she could demand again, this time
to see Señor Delgadillo, since it didn't look as though
Rolfe was here, he was continuing, 'I arrived from my
ranch in Durango today anticipating being a guest at
Graciela's marriage tomorrow.'

'Anticipating . . .?'

The way he said it, it was almost as if he was
intimating that there wasn't going to be a wedding
tomorrow. But that was ridiculous; the arrangements
had been made two months ago at least, to her certain
knowledge.

Hauteur was still with her when, ready to do some
ignoring of her own, she questioned, 'Might I see
Graciela or one of her family?'

'Did you not understand me?' he enquired coolly; she
knew he knew very well she had. 'I have just told you *I*
am family.'

'I meant a more *immediate* member of the family.'

Those eyes were narrowing again, giving her a fair

idea that she had come somewhere near to insulting him. She was sure of it as his cool manner left him.

'I don't know about your country,' she was told cuttingly, 'but in my country, Mexico,' all the confirmation there in that proud statement that he was indeed Mexican, 'when trouble hits one member of the family we unite as one, no matter how distant the relationship.'

'Trouble?' The arrogance, the pride in the man was sinking her. 'What trouble?' she asked, hauteur gone, her voice quiet.

'My name is Javier Zarazua Guerrero,' he told her formally, her second question going unanswered. 'My cousin Carlos has asked me to deal with you. He, his wife, and Graciela have had enough of the Shearman family to last them for a very long time.'

'Enough of the . . .' Weariness was grabbing at her again. She was making not the least bit of sense of any of this. This chilling man had been asked to deal with her! She tried hard to get herself together. Since this man wasn't giving her any answers, all she could hope was to see Rolfe as soon as possible—he could soon clear everything up.

'Then perhaps, Señor Guerrero . . .'

'Zarazua,' he corrected.

'Then perhaps, *señor*, since it is you *I* am to deal with, you will tell me the address of my brother's house, then I need trouble you no further.' She saw a hardening of the ice in him, but went bravely on, trying to ignore that he was getting colder by the second. 'I called at Rolfe's flat and was told he had moved out. In his last letter to me he said he had purchased a house for himself and Gr . . .'

'He has purchased *nothing*. The house that was to be the future home of Graciela was bought for them by her father. Not one peso did your brother contribute to the property.'

And while she was gasping, for she was sure the inference in Rolfe's letter was that *he* had bought it, Javier Zarazua was ramming home:

'Your brother, Señorita Shearman, was interested in only one thing from his *novia*.' Colour flooded her face, and that colour turned a deeper red, when, observing her, Javier Zarazua snarled, 'Not *that*. He was receiving that from another source. As far as Graciela was concerned, the only interest Shearman had in her was the money he thought she would one day inherit. Unwisely—or wisely as I see it—the child yesterday revealed to him that the firm he was under the impression her father owns belongs to me, that Carlos had no money other than what I pay him to manage the business for me.'

Her colour was ashen as he flailed to an end. 'Rolfe—Rolfe isn't interested in money,' she said faintly. 'He never has been. I don't . . .'

'Don't believe it?' The words were said like a whiplash; her calling him a liar was not going down very well, she saw. 'Then believe this, *señorita*. This morning, on the eve of his wedding, your *un*mercenary brother saw fit to jilt his *novia*.'

'Jilt!' she echoed, her head swimming with what was being said, her reeling senses not being helped by the fact that she hadn't seen a bed for over twenty-four hours. 'I can't . . .'

'Not only did he jilt her when he discovered his expectations of being a wealthy man were without foundation. He had the unmitigated impertinence to add insult to injury by taking with him a woman he must have been seeing while having the audacity to pay court here.'

Cally was on her feet. 'No!' she shouted, and 'No!' again.

But her voice was not so strong the second time. Her energy seemed to be draining from her. Blankly she stared at him, trying to shut her mind off from anything else terrible he had to say as she saw his mouth move grimly as he accused, 'And if you've chased over here to see what pickings there are in it for you . . .' And she just couldn't take any more.

She made to take a step—where, she knew not, then discovered as her legs began to buckle that all her strength had gone, making the only move possible a downward one towards the carpet. She was still looking at his fierce face when her vision blurred. She thought vaguely that she saw a minimum of concern there that was at odds with his previous expression. Then as her knees folded, she thought not of another thing—her last conscious remembrance that of strong arms coming suddenly to hold her.

CHAPTER TWO

CALLY came round in the same room in which she had fainted. But the strong arms that had come round her were no longer there, causing her to wonder, as her eyelids fluttered open to see Javier Zarazua stooping beside her, if she had imagined he had made a speedy grab to catch her.

Perhaps not, she thought, though he must have handled her somehow since she was comfortably stretched out on a couch, and not in a heap on the floor.

Lassitude gripped. It had her wanting to close her eyes again. And then memory of the terrible things this taller than most Mexicans she had seen had said to her had her struggling to sit up, struggling to hold on to what dignity she could. Once she had found Rolfe she would be able to refute all this arrogant man's charges.

'You are feeling better, *señorita?*'

She thought his tone was particularly lacking in solicitude. Then she recalled what had sounded muzzy in her head at the time. He had accused her of chasing to Mexico to see what pickings there were for her!

'I'm perfectly well,' she told him frigidly, not doubting now that his lack of solicitude was due to the fact that he hadn't believed in her faint anyway.

Cally thanked God then for her pride that ignored lassitude and had her standing, nothing about her showing how rocky she was feeling on her feet. The man she was beginning to hate more than she had hated any other individual was on his feet too. But she moved

away from the hand that came out and looked to be
going to steady her.

'I apologise for passing out like that,' she said stiffly.
'It's not something I normally do—It—it's some time
since I have slept.'

'Permit me, *señorita*, to remedy that.'

She looked at him, her brain clearing by the minute,
the unenviable position she was in fast being born in
her. She hadn't any idea where her brother was. Neither
apparently had anyone else. She had very little money,
nowhere near enough for her fare home.

'You are suggesting I sleep here?'

'Hardly,' he told her coldly. 'My family are suffering
enough at the hands of your family. It is unthinkable
that Graciela should wake from her sedation on the day
that should have been her wedding day and find her
betrayer's sister sleeping under her roof.'

'Rolfe wouldn't . . .' Even if she had known what she
could say to defend her absent brother, Cally found she
didn't get the chance.

'I will take you to a hotel. We will go now.'

So he didn't want her in the house a minute longer.
She could understand that, she supposed, if Graciela
had had to receive medical attention to calm her. Yet
she couldn't believe Rolfe had done what he stood
accused of. He had sounded so much in love in his
letter, had been looking forward to his wedding day.

'You are ready?'

She had to leave her thoughts on Rolfe and the
plaguing question of what was the true story behind all
this. More important was that she should concentrate
on her own predicament.

Without answering she picked up the small travel bag
she had brought in with her and moved to the door she
had come in by. Javier Zarazua was right there with
her, ushering her through, going with her along the

terrace where he collected her cases and took her to a
car parked along the avenue.

'One moment,' he said tersely, and left her to go back
inside the house—either to tell Señor and Señora
Delgadillo what was happening, she thought, or to tell
the maid to bolt the door behind him.

He was soon back—and not inclined to conversation,
which suited her very well. In his absence she had done
a quick mental check on her money, and was anxiously
hoping he had it in mind to select some small
inexpensive hotel.

Her heart sank when he drew up at a large, smart
modern hotel. It was going to cost the earth, she knew
it.

'I would prefer somewhere smaller.' She hoped he
would think her protest arose from nothing more than
that she just didn't like large, smart modern hotels.

'What you prefer is of little importance to me,' he
told her uncivilly, already opening his door. 'It is late. I
do not intend to spend half the night looking for
something more suited to your taste.'

He had a case in either hand, was standing on the
pavement obviously expecting her not to question his
authority. He was obviously waiting for her to precede
him into the hotel, but Cally wasn't moving a step.

And she hated him more—hated him, because of
what he had said about her being there for the pickings,
because she was going to have to tell him something of
her financial position.

Still on that pavement, ready to get back into his car,
she faced him, and woodenly told him, 'My—funds
don't run to this sort of hotel.'

'You are here without money?'

She didn't like at all the satisfaction in his voice that
said she had confirmed his worst suspicions. Without
her looking at him, again pride had her sticking her

head in the air, this time to march forward into the hotel foyer. Not one word more did she intend to speak to him. It would cripple her financially to stay here, she knew it. But she would think about that when she'd had some sleep.

She stood to one side while he conversed with the man on reception, and she wasn't waiting for anything when a bellboy took her cases and the key from the receptionist. Looking straight through Javier Zarazua Guerrero, though not unaware of the glint that was in his eyes as he saw her intention, she cut him dead, and with her back ramrod-stiff, she marched in the wake of the bellboy to the lift.

Sunlight was streaming through her window when she awakened. Cally checked her watch—she had thought she had been tired enough to sleep for days, yet it was only ten to eight. Though she was surprised she had slept at all with the weight of worries she had on her mind. But remembering the exhaustion that had enveloped her the moment the bellboy had gone, perhaps it wasn't so surprising sleep had claimed her the moment her head had hit the pillow. An unexpected attack of coughing took her, making her eyes water. She was here in the sun now, so why hadn't her cough gone? she wondered. Then she had no time for such whimsical thoughts, as she came wide awake, other thoughts crowding in, and the bed that last night had held such appeal was vacated.

She was coming from her shower, dressed in a many times washed though still presentable cotton frock, when she saw the hotel notice stating that rooms had to be vacated by two o'clock.

That meant she had until two to make up her mind what she was going to do. Well, for a start she was going to go along to see that landlord Tim had spoken with last night. Somehow she had to make herself understood. Surely if Rolfe had flitted off with some woman, though she didn't believe that for an instant, he would have left some indication of where he was going?

Knowing she had to be careful with her money, Cally opened one of the two bottles of mineral water that reposed on the dressing table, and hydrated her insides with that rather than the excellent coffee she was sure the hotel served.

The hot sun she found welcome at first, but within ten minutes of walking, she was soon realising it was no good going anywhere at full pelt, and was thankful to rest for five minutes in one of the many squares Querétaro held.

It was with the help of her phrase book and the letter with Rolfe's address on, not to mention the hand language of the policeman she approached to show her the way, that after a further half an hour of walking, of facing the hazards of tearaway traffic as she crossed pink quarrystone streets, she eventually made it to the building she had last night visited with Julie and Tim.

It was a listless Cally who had to admit defeat when after ringing the doorbell repeatedly, knocking loudly on the door, although she could hear the bell was in working order, she came away from the building not knowing where she was going and hardly caring. She'd have to come back, of course. But a fresh problem was now presenting itself, kept at bay while thinking that if she had Rolfe's new address she would easily find him. Where on earth was she going to sleep that night?

Hot, bothered, and not a little scared, she found herself in Madero Street and took the opportunity to get out of the sun by diving into Woolworths. She had no intention of buying anything, but it was cooler in there and she spent minutes in studying the cards in the picture postcard rack, her mind a jumble of what did she do now?

She was no clearer in her mind when she replaced the card of the many, many arched aqueduct she had been driven under last night, and went outside again. Nearby there was another square, with a water fountain tinkling, and many other people electing to take their ease on the benches placed in the area.

Too restless to sit for long, Cally was soon on her feet again, but her feet were in no hurry. Querétaro, she knew, was a place of great historic interest. It was here that the Emperor Maximilian had been executed. Here where Josefa Ortiz de Dominguez, La Corregidora, heroine of the Independence, had lived, her remains brought back to Querétaro after her death. Ambling on, not looking for the statue of that brave lady, by accident Cally came across it, and couldn't help but wish she felt anywhere near as brave.

But she wasn't feeling brave, she felt anything but brave as she moved on. She felt scared and alone. The last thing she could do was to appeal to the Delgadillo family for help. And never would she ask that Javier Zarazua for anything! Not that she would be seeing him again. He had dumped her in a hotel, and as far as he was concerned, that was her finished with.

It had gone twelve when, while not hurrying, she seemed to have spent most of the morning in walking. Cally came to the church of Santa Rosa. The gold baroque interior she found too much to take in, but she came out feeling marginally calmer, though still worried as she went in to sit in the beautiful square that faced the church.

She was reminded of time when she looked at the church clock, although both faces showed that the clock had stopped, one reading half past four, while the small hand was missing on the other face, the large hand on six. She had to be back at her hotel before two, she knew, but she wasn't looking forward to picking up her two suitcases and lugging them around with her. Her mind flitted on to wonder if she could get some sort of job to keep her until she could scrape enough together for her fare home. But she had no idea what sort of work permit she would need to work in Mexico. And anyway, what sort of work could she do? All she knew was how to keep house, and anybody could do that.

Her eyes attracted to a splash of colour, she left her worries for a brief moment, gazing with pleasure at the beautiful flowering bougainvillaea growing on a nearby wall. She loved flowers, and was lost for a moment as she looked at the beauty her eyes beheld. So she was in no way prepared for the hard aggression that ripped into her ears from a voice she had thought never to hear again.

'And just where in sweet hell do you think you've been?'

Shock at seeing an angry chin thrust forward and Javier Zarazua standing over her made her instinctively reel back in fear. That was until she recalled that it was he who had told those terrible lies about Rolfe. She made herself sit still, a remoteness in her face, easily obtained since she was naturally reserved anyway.

'Your command of the English language amazes me,' she told him coolly, trying not to notice that he didn't appear to be having much success if that taut look meant he was trying to control his temper. 'I *know* where I've been,' she added, still endeavouring to stay cool. 'I went to see my brother's landlord.'

'What for?'

She had just decided he could mind his own business, when he moved to come and share the white-painted iron fretwork bench with her. She didn't like him this close, though it was preferable to having him standing in front glaring at her.

'I went to enquire his address.'

'I could have saved you the trouble.'

Her head spun round. 'You know where he is?' For a moment she forgot to be cool, her grey-green eyes alive, a fact observed with the coolness she had lost by her adversary. 'His ex-landlord wasn't in when I went—I was going to go again later today when I thought he would be home from work.'

'No, I don't know where he is. I wish I did,' Javier Zarazua told her shortly, his look telling her it would bode ill for Rolfe if ever he did catch up with him. 'Gonzalez, the landlord, doesn't know where he went either.'

Cally felt herself begin to crumble. She admitted only then that she had been pinning all her hopes on the landlord knowing where Rolfe had gone, of maybe telephoning him if he was out of Querétaro and telling him of her dire straits. But with that threat in the Mexican's voice telling her what he was ready to do to Rolfe the minute he clapped eyes on him, she just had to believe he was telling the truth.

'Thank you for saving me a second journey,' she said primly, and stood up. But she had taken only a few paces when a hand descended on her arm, halting her.

'And just where do you think you're off to now?'

She tried to shake that hard band of iron off her arm, but it didn't work. She was near to tears, but didn't want him to have the further satisfaction of seeing that.

'I'm going to my hotel to collect my cases and settle my account,' she said—then found she was going nowhere but back to the seat she had just vacated if she didn't want an ungainly struggle with everyone watching.

'Your hotel bill is already settled,' Javier Zarazua fired her anger by telling her the moment they were seated.

'You settled it!' He let go her arm as indignantly she

pulled so she could open her bag. 'If you'll kindly tell me how much——' she began affronted, rooting for her thin wallet.

'Don't be ridiculous!' he snapped, and she saw then he was offended that right there in full view of other people sitting around she was offering to give him money. Well, he wasn't the only one to have pride, she thought, not seeing why it should be all right for him to think he could offend her and then get uptight that she should offend him.

'I'm not being ridiculous,' she snapped right back. 'But if it offends your manly pride to . . .'

The look on his face stopped her—he looked ready to slap her! She saw the movement of his jaw, then knew she had been wrong about his vanity. For right there, careless of anyone's opinion of him, he told her how much her overnight accommodation had cost. And while she was trying not to blanch at the figure he quoted, he held out his hand for reimbursement.

He had sharp eyes too, evidently. As she held her wallet in her hand, he saw for himself, when she emptied it of notes, just how much money she had at her disposal.

'I'll take it in traveller's cheques if that's all the loose change you have,' he offered magnanimously.

Loose change! The notes in her hand represented all her wealth. 'I don't have traveller's cheques,' she muttered, and knew herself heard when he asked:

'Does that amount there constitute your whole fortune?'

'I can afford to pay my own hotel account,' she said stiffly, getting angry that he was making no move to take the money she was offering. It was almost as if the only reason he had said he would take the money from her was just so he could see inside her wallet for himself how much money she had. She wished she hadn't told him about not having any traveller's cheques too, and felt such a fool sitting there pushing the money at him, only to be ignored.

He deigned to flick a glance at the money she held out to him, and she knew, as the limited amount of her resources was registered, that she had just confirmed for him that she *was* there for the pickings. It was there in his voice, unveiled sarcasm dripping as he asked:

'How long did you say you were staying?'

'I expected to find my brother here,' she said coldly, something he already knew, but her only defence.

'You expected him to finance your stay?'

'I—He invited me to come. He said . . .' Oh, why bother! Pride was with her again. 'I can just as easily go home again,' she lied.

'You have your return flight booked?' he asked sharply—so sharply, that unaccustomed to lying, Cally was replying before she had time to think.

'No—Well—no.'

'But you do have a return ticket?'

Her sudden high colour gave her away, and she knew by the way he was looking at her that he had read her answer from her blush.

'I can get a job—work. I . . .'

'You were expecting your brother to pay your return fare?'

'Out of his own money, not Gr . . . Not his ex-fiancée's.'

She wondered how much chance she had of getting up and leaving without his brute force coming to stop her, if she tried it again. But at that moment she was so overcome by the lassitude she had experienced last night, she had to wonder if that unusual 'flu virus she had picked up was still lurking in her system.

'It seems to me,' said Javier Zarazua, having been silent for some moments, 'that you, Señorita Shearman, are, to put it mildly, in something of what I think could safely be termed a mess.'

She didn't need him to tell her that—and didn't thank him for it either. 'Now aren't you the bright one?' she said, finding a cool sarcasm of her own. She would leave him in a minute, would risk his grabbing hold of her arm again, though why he should, she couldn't think.

'I don't think it too wise for you to take that tone with me, *señorita*.' His voice was hard, with a warning note there. He hadn't liked her sarcasm, her coolness either, she knew.

'Why?' she challenged insolently. All her life she had been put in her place by her father—in her opinion, it was more than time she stood up for herself.

'Because, Cally Shearman, while I can guarantee no one hereabouts will employ you——' he paused, watched while some of the arrogance went out of her as his remark sank in, saw in her eyes she wasn't quick enough to divert from the chipped blue ice in his the desperation his comment wrought in her, then continued, 'there is a chance I may consider employing you.'

That jolted her, her eyes going huge as she stared at him, startled, and saw he looked to be serious. Then she was hating herself this time that while given the option he would be the last man she would consider working for, she was all too well aware that she was in 'a mess', and needed money so badly she was going to have to swallow her pride and find out more.

'What—sort of a job?' she asked painfully, her pride flattened, looking away.

'What sort of work did you do in England?'

Housekeeping had come naturally to her, she hadn't had any choice. No housekeeper her father had employed in those early days after her mother's death

had put up with his parsimonious ways for very long.
She had gravitated to the job naturally.

'I didn't go out to work,' she said wearily, knowing
she was back to square one. Who was going to employ
her when she had no experience of work outside her
own home?

'You preferred to live in idleness?' he broke in before
she could tell him she had kept house for her father.
And not allowing her to interrupt and tell him that
apart from two days in bed when she had collapsed
with 'flu, she had spent very few idle moments in that
big old-fashioned house, he was sarcastically asking,
'What sort of work were you hoping to get to earn your
fare to England?'

'Housework—hotel work—anything. The job wasn't
important.'

Silence fell as he took that without any further
sarcastic offering. Then if he had been making a
decision whether or not to go back on his suggestion
that he might employ her, his mind was suddenly made
up, and he, as though he was already her employer, was
firing orders at her, very much the one on top.

'Put your money away, you'll need all of that and
more. We will lunch first, then I will take you with me to
Durango.'

'*Durango!*'

'It is where I live. I have already told you that,' he
told her sharply as if it offended him to repeat himself.
'You have stated you will do housework—I have the
very thing for you.'

'Housework?' she questioned, loathing him, but
ready to grab at anything, though a streak of caution
held her back from going anywhere with him until she
knew more about it.

'You were hoping for something less—menial,
perhaps?' His sarcasm hadn't stayed down for very

long. And if her arrogance had annoyed him earlier,
then he was getting his own back now as loftily he
looked down his nose and suggested, 'Perhaps you had
thought, working in a hotel, to meet someone wealthy
the way your brother thought he had?' And at her
sharply indrawn breath, 'Are you afraid to soil your
hands with nothing more at the end of it than your air
fare back to where you came from?'

Pride surfaced, and she held on to it. 'I'm not
afraid of hard work,' she stated, that coldness back
with her. 'I merely require to know more. More of—
of the job I am to do. I know very little of you,
señor. I think you will agree, it's natural I should
want . . .'

'You think I am taking you into my home in order to
have—my way—with you?' His eyes looked her over as
though he despised what he saw, then, 'Permit me to
tell you,' he said, his voice besting hers when it came to
sub-zero temperature, 'that my taste runs to women
with more flesh on their bones.'

Cally had to take his insult to her slender frame, even
if privately she thought her figure wasn't all that bad.
She had good legs and curved nicely in all the right
places, she had thought. Then she left private thought
as another thought his remark had put into her head
made itself known.

'I had not thought for an instant that your—er—
feelings were that way inclined,' she primly set him
straight. 'If anything had occurred to me at all, it was
only to reflect why you should ask me to be your
housekeeper, when it's obvious we neither of us like
the other.' It was putting what she did feel for him
mildly, but her pride was mollified by letting him
know that if he was drowning she might, just, throw
him a lifebelt, though it was as far as she dared go still
hopeful, since it was Hobson's choice, that he might

take her on. 'But what concerns me more is, will your
wife be agreeable to . . .'

'I have no wife.'

His blunt statement had her looking into those
extraordinary blue eyes. From the look of him, he
appeared to be quite happy to be a bachelor. And from
that sensuous curve to his bottom lip, a far from
celibate bachelor at that. Quickly she brought her mind
away from such thoughts.

'I would have to live with you in your house?' she
questioned, hoping with everything she had that he
wasn't going to say yes, hoping that he wasn't going to
say it would be just him and her there. It would be
murder. He hated her for what Rolfe had done to his
family—hated her because of his conviction that she
had only come to Mexico to see what was in it for her—
and she just knew sparks would fly whenever they came
into contact. For having discovered her new-found
freedom, she had no intention of leaving the tyrant her
father had been, only to submissively subject herself to
everything this fresh tyrant would throw at her.

'You will live with me under my roof,' he told her at
last, taking his time about putting her out of her misery.
And seeing for himself that the idea hadn't exactly sent
her into raptures, he drawled slowly, 'But you will be
adequately chaperoned,' and a sarcastic, 'if that worries
you in any way,' his tone clearly indicating that he
knew her sort, and that it wouldn't bother her one bit
whether there was a chaperone there or not. 'My
housekeeper and her husband live on the premises.' His
cold tone faded as a smile Cally didn't believe in
showed itself. 'So even should I so far forget that a
skinned rabbit has more meat, then you may sleep
soundly in your bed, *señorita*. Teresa in particular, and
Arturo her husband, would frown very heavily to
have—er—naughty goings on in the house.'

More insults! More laying it on the line that she was the last woman he would fancy, and Cally felt a tinge of pique mingle with the relief that should have been two hundred per cent. She knew little of men, but she wasn't so dim she couldn't tell an admiring glance if she saw one, and she hadn't done the household shopping without receiving one or two of those on the way. It dawned on her then that Javier Zarazua was trying to undermine her confidence in herself, trying to take her down a peg or two. She wasn't likely to tell him that half her arrogance was all part and parcel of her natural reserve, that many times she had wanted to be friendly to people, only that spontaneity in her had been part way flattened. Only here in Mexico, in that coach last night, had she started to come out of her shell.

She left her thoughts and pinned her mind to what else he had said. He was giving her all the time she needed to dwell on it.

Having until a few days ago been a very efficient housekeeper—her father would tolerate no other—she had foolishly assumed when Javier Zarazua had said she would do housework that he was offering her a job as his housekeeper. But if this pious-sounding Teresa was his housekeeper, what then was Cally's role to be in his household?

'Am I to understand that I'm to do the rough work in your house?' She asked the question her intelligence already had the answer to. It had come to her, as she sat stiffly on that iron bench, that the only reason he had for helping her out of the 'mess' she was in stemmed in no way whatever from any philanthropic attitude. He hated her for what her brother had done to a member of his family, and he was out to make her pay—the hard way.

'You will be working in my house. Sleeping there, yes.' And he smiled, and she looked away, an endorsement in that sardonic smile, if she needed one, that no one got uppity with him and got away with it—without him having the added debt to settle with her family. He thought she had been a lady of leisure who didn't know one end of a scrubbing brush from the other—it would delight him to see her down on her knees. 'The job I have for you, Cally Shearman, is to thoroughly clean the house of the new overseer I am expecting to arrive shortly.'

Cally favoured him with a smile of her own; housework and she were old acquaintances. 'I don't expect that will take me very long,' she told him with an air of, 'Now try something else you think will horrify me.' Because that hadn't horrified her one bit. And still smiling, hoping to soon lose this feeling of tiredness and be raring to roll her sleeves up and show him. 'But I really couldn't take all my air fare from you for less than a week's work.'

It was his turn to smile, and her own smile faded. 'If in the event that particular work is completed, to my satisfaction,' a none too gentle hint there that every corner of the house would be inspected, 'before you have earned your air fare, then I have no doubt at all that I shall be able to find you something similar to do.'

Cally had visions of being made to scrub out every building that stood on his ranch before her plane eventually took off for England.

And she had thought her father was a tyrant!

CHAPTER THREE

DURANGO lay at the foothills of the Sierra Madre. And there was only one word to describe the spot where Javier Zarazua had his ranch, and that word was—beautiful.

Having flown from Querétaro in a private plane, they had then driven for about an hour and a half after arriving in the state capital. But Cally had been in no mood then to appreciate the scenic delights of colourful rocks, lush tree-covered hills, pine and oak in abundance.

Nor did she have any mind the following morning, as she sat beside Javier in his car being driven to his new overseer's house, to appreciate the opportunity to live for a short time among such splendour. She wanted out—and as quickly as possible.

Her employer, for that was how she regarded the now casually dressed man by her side, appeared to have nothing he wanted to say to her; and had been barely civil to her ever since the moment she had agreed to go with him. He had known, of course, that she would accept his offer—what choice had she?

Under such circumstances, she felt it natural that she should be cool with him. The things he had said about Rolfe still niggled. The things he had thought, and *said*, about her were not conducive to thawing out that reserve that had grown up with her. But if she was treating him with a certain degree of coldness, then his attitude with her was downright arctic.

She remembered their arrival yesterday, as dusk began to descend—remembered the way she had gone to collect her cases, only to be barked at for her trouble, 'Leave them. Arturo will take them to your room.'

He then strode in front of her into his superbly appointed house, leaving her to follow quickly if she didn't want to get lost as she entered under an archway where she saw there was a veritable maze of openings and doors.

He called, 'Teresa!' and a well covered woman any number of years past fifty had appeared. Her skin was that shade of brown Cally had seen showing the mixture of Indian and Spanish blood, unlike Javier Zarazua's skin which in contrast was a light bronze. Her dress too was dark, its only relief the silver cross hanging from her neck.

But the employer of them both lost his uncivil manner when addressing the forbidding-looking Teresa. He spoke to her in Spanish, and Cally, catching the word *'señorita'*, was fairly certain he was saying something about her.

She had thought from the way he had been with her that the courtesy of an introduction might be done away with, and had consequently had to hide her surprise when he turned and performed that formality, his manner in front of his housekeeper marginally warmer before, the shaking of hands over, he confirmed that he had been talking to Teresa about her, by saying:

'Teresa has a room prepared for you,' leaving her to guess, as he turned to speak to Teresa again, at what stage since she had agreed to go with him he had contacted her, because she couldn't recall him letting her out of his sight from that moment. But there was no time to ponder, for he was again coming over her employer, and telling her, 'Teresa will show you to your room. We dine in half an hour.'

About to follow the dark-clad figure who was already

on her way, Cally hesitated, her mind fixed on that 'We'.

'I'm to dine with your staff?' she questioned, not liking that 'We' one little bit. If it was left to her, she much preferred to eat in the servants' quarters.

He surveyed her with that superior arrogant look she thoroughly detested. 'You will take your meals with me.'

'But . . .'

'Your presence in Teresa's kitchen will embarrass her,' he cut in, causing her to think, save your breath, Cally, and to realise she had a lot to learn about Mexican ways, having no idea, since she was a servant too, why her presence in the kitchen should embarrass anyone. Well, one thing she knew, she had had enough of the domineering Javier Zarazua for today! To sit across the table from him at dinner was more than she was prepared to take.

'You will excuse me, *señor*,' she said, her reserve showing in her stiff politeness, 'but I'm not at all hungry.'

'You ate little at lunch.'

'My appetite has always been small.'

That caused his eyes to rake over her, caused her to expect any second some other disagreeable comment on what he saw as her thinness. But, a master at surprising her, he surprised her again.

'Go with Teresa,' he clipped, seemed to hesitate himself, then added, 'She has no English; if there is anything you are short of, come to me.'

Cally turned from him, thinking she would do without rather than ask him for anything. Though since he couldn't stand the sight of her either, she was puzzled that he should suggest, if everything in her room wasn't as it should be, that she should go to him.

The room Teresa took her to was white, cool, and

airy. A soft breeze fluttered at the open window. The large bed with its carved Mexican headboard and matching lower footboard looked temptingly inviting. Teresa did not stay many seconds, but unsmilingly received her, 'Gracias, Teresa.'

And it was with a polite, 'Con permiso,' that she left her to it.

As soon as she had gone, Cally investigated the adjoining bathroom—and couldn't help but think that for a servant of the Señor she had a very luxurious apartment indeed. But lord, she felt tired! She had been dogged by tiredness ever since she had set foot on Mexican soil, or so it seemed. Thinking perhaps a bath might work wonders, and putting her tiredness down to the fact that she hadn't yet acclimatised, and must now be somewhere about six thousand feet above sea level, she shut herself in the bathroom.

Somewhat refreshed from her bath, she saw that in her absence her cases had been brought to her room. But by the time she had unpacked, she was tired again, and decided that that inviting-looking bed was where she was heading. Then she discovered her surprises for the day were not yet over.

Before she could make it to the bed, a knock summoned her to her door, where she saw the unsmiling Teresa standing there holding a tray. If Javier Zarazua had sent up her dinner determined to fatten her up, she thought, taking the tray from the sombre Teresa, then she could be sure it was more because he wanted some work out of her tomorrow than because he liked his women with more meat on them.

Cally wondered now, as he drew up outside a house that looked neglected, as though no one had lived in it for years, if she should thank him for seeing that the condemned lady ate a hearty meal, although she had eaten little of it, sleep soon claiming her. She decided against it and followed him out to the car. If he had been on a diet of limes—a favourite with Tequila, Rolfe had written her—for a year, then he couldn't be more sour than he was this morning.

'Take this,' he ordered shortly, when she would have walked from him and investigated the house.

Cally turned. 'This' was a cardboard box. She took it from him, then stood waiting while he extracted a larger, heavier box, and a picnic basket, then extracted a long-handled sweeping brush she hadn't noticed.

'I think you have all the cleaning materials here you will need,' he said without much charm, then left her to follow him as he unlocked the stout padlock on the door of the house, that goodness knew where its neighbour was, for she couldn't see another house in sight.

Her first glance at the interior was enough to have her efficient housekeeping soul wince. The place was filthy! And she had thought to have it spick and span in under a week! Her thoughts went on as without a word being spoken she was shown from room to room. She'd be lucky to have it the way she wanted it in under a month!

'By the look of it, my air fare is going to be hard earned.' The comment just wouldn't stay down as they reached the kitchen and she saw the grease and dirt-stained cooker that looked as though it was going to occupy one complete day on its own.

She thought she saw disgust in his eyes too, but whether for her or the state of the place, she couldn't tell. Though she thought maybe there was a semblance of an apology in his, 'Vandals used this place as their headquarters for some weeks after the previous occupants left,' before she decided he wasn't apologising at all when his glance went to her hands, then to her pale face, and his jaw jutted. 'I will call for you at four.'

And abruptly as he left her. 'Get started.'

Where to start? The whole place was a pigsty. Left to herself, Cally looked over every room again. Dead leaves and litter were everywhere. Furniture that looked as though it had once known a loving hand was now dull, lifeless, dirty and festooned with grease marks. Cally 'got started'.

Weariness was her companion by the time she had swept from top to bottom, that same lassitude she had experienced of late coming to slow her. An attack of coughing drained her, causing her to break off.

Memory of the taunt, 'Are you afraid to soil your hands' had her digging in her heels when she would have loved to have sat down. Instead she gathered up the rubbish she had accumulated and unbolted the back door.

Brilliant sunshine greeted her, had her leaving the rubbish outside and investigating the area where she decided the weekly wash was done. There were two deep sinks, she saw, but a cold tap only. Determined not to be beaten, she fought against tiredness, and went back inside to take down the curtains from the upstairs room, then went to put them in soak.

By the time the weighty curtains were washed a few hours later, Cally felt near to a state of exhaustion. Her movements heavy, she re-bolted the back door, strapped on her watch and just had to go and sit down.

The wooden-armed settee beneath her, she hung on while the world spun crazily. Common sense told her she might feel better if she could get down some of the food in the hamper—but just the thought of food nauseated her.

Thinking to rest for a moment, she pulled her feet up on to the settee, her mind drifting to consider that, although she felt leaden, she had spent quite a useful day. The upstairs was starting to take shape. She would concentrate on that region this week. That meant of course that when Javier Zarazua showed his sour face at four o'clock it would look as though she had done nothing all day but sweep the leaves from the downstairs rooms. But, since she didn't doubt he would wander over the whole house doing an inspection, he would soon see she hadn't spent very many minutes in idleness. He would see too, though she doubted as she yawned that men noted such things—her father never had—that she hadn't had time to stop for lunch.

She stirred, realised she must have nodded off for a second, and opened her eyes. And then colour came surging to her face. She flicked a glance at her watch, then back to the grim-faced man who had come silently in while she—had been fast asleep.

'I . . .' she gasped, not having meant to nod off, then, regaining speech, 'It's only half past three!'

'And you, you idle bitch, weren't expecting me until four,' he grated toughly, his eyes flicking round to see the place still looked as though pigs might find it a happy abode.

'I . . .' Cally began again—and found he wasn't interested in excuses, wasn't interested as she had supposed in investigating farther than his eyes could see of what she had achieved that day.

'Come,' he said sharply, looking ready to tip her out of the settee if she didn't move herself. Then as she left the settee and Javier Zarazua took up the picnic hamper, she saw a sudden devilish light appear in his eyes. 'Work as fast as you have today, and you will never earn that plane ticket, Cally Shearman,' he mocked.

For answer she pushed her nose in the air and walked straight past him, for the first time in her life feeling her hand itch with the urge to take a swing at someone.

By the time they reached the homestead, the cold fury

in her had dipped slightly, though she was still quietly seething, determined to work until she dropped tomorrow, the sooner to leave this hostile place, as absently she followed him when he went to the rear of the house and entered through the kitchen to deposit the food hamper.

A girl of about her own age turned from washing dishes as they went in, a dot of a black-haired child clinging to her, immediately burying her face in the girl's skirts.

Javier halted, causing Cally to have to halt too if she didn't want to go cannoning into him as he paused. She heard Teresa's name mentioned as he addressed the girl, and the word 'siesta', and guessed he was asking if Teresa was resting.

'Si, señor,' the girl answered.

'Bueno,' he replied, and seemed only then to realise Cally was right there with him—which had him introducing the girl Rosa, and her child Rosalinda, who at his coaxing—another surprise to see such a human streak in him—came out from her mother's skirts.

Rosa's smile was instant and friendly as Cally extended her hand. And feeling warmth that had so far been absent, the reserve in her just wouldn't stand up. Her own smile was much in evidence when under the mother's instructions the little black-haired doll child came to shake hands too, smiles crossing the language barrier as the child repeated after her mother, 'Mucho gusto, señorita.'

Cally was just straightening up after bending to the tiny tot, when she caught the eyes of Javier Zarazua on her face, and that was the end of her smile. She hadn't missed something in his expression that said he was having difficulty in connecting the lazy slob he had just found sleeping on the job—having mistaken her reserve for snobbishness like everyone else, she wouldn't wonder—with a girl who could look pleased to pass the time of day with the maid's child.

'*Excusi,*' she said to Rosa, knowing somewhere along the line she was getting her non-existent Spanish mixed up with her non-existent Italian, although it looked as though the still smiling Rosa knew what she was trying to say. Discovering there was sufficient space now for her to get by without having to touch the hard-eyed man who was still looking at her, Cally went from the kitchen.

Since she was unfamiliar with the layout of the house, it was more by luck than good judgment that she found the stairs that led to her room. Hoping she wouldn't have to see her never give her credit for anything employer again that day, she had in fact reached the door of her room, when suddenly he was right there beside her.

She halted, because he wasn't going on to his room, wherever it lay, but had stopped too, to say something unpleasant, she didn't doubt. And, weary again, her temper that had seldom had an airing growing nearer and nearer the surface, she knew that if he said just one word about the small amount of work he thought she had done that day, then that itch in her right palm might have its way. It was getting more and more out of control the longer he took to study her.

'You are looking tired,' he said, ever a man with surprises. 'Might I suggest you follow Teresa's example and rest for a while?'

Amazement at this turnabout, this change in him very nearly had her agreeing that she would love to do nothing better. But she couldn't forget in a hurry that he had called her an idle bitch; it dug into her, so that she did not thank him for his suggestion.

'Anything else?' she queried, her voice haughty, and saw the ice forming in his eyes for her trouble. So she wasn't altogether surprised when he rapped:

'Dinner is at eight.'

'At the risk of repeating myself, I'm not hungry.'

She thought then that her arrogance grated on him as much as his arrogance grated on her, and saw from the flame that flared briefly in his eyes that she wasn't mistaken. She noted the way his right hand clenched, and quailed inside that it looked as if he also had face-slapping itches. But he had control too, it seemed, for slowly that clenched hand unfurled, though his voice was about as cool as molten lava when he said:

'Then go without. You have had one good meal today. I do not intend that Teresa should fetch and carry for the likes of you.'

He strode from her, a fine fury showing in his steel-plated back, before Cally could tell him it was his idea that Teresa brought her dinner to her room last night, not hers. That he was under the impression she had eaten everything that food hamper housed was unimportant.

She should, Cally thought the next day when she had worked so that she was bathed in perspiration, have been overjoyed to find each day as sunny as the previous one. But, roasting alive as she sent the iron backwards and forwards over the curtains she had washed yesterday, she would have welcomed the winter temperature to be found in her old home.

As she had been unable to run an ironing board to earth, the kitchen table having a varnished top and not being suitable either, her task was made more difficult in that she used the mattress on one of the beds as an ironing base.

The exhaustion that had become familiar was back with her when at last she unplugged the iron. She was sure it must be the altitude that was knocking her sideways as she left the newly ironed curtains draped across the bed so they shouldn't collect creases, to go down to the kitchen to collect the curtain fixing that had had to be scrubbed.

Her footsteps, tired and listless, were silent and incapable of hurrying as she went slowly down stairs. She was through the wide hallway when a small sensation of shock took her, her nerves quickly calming as she saw that the man standing with his back to her in the kitchen was Javier Zarazua. She had no idea of the time, her watch was upstairs somewhere, but she would have thought, if she hadn't heard his car, she would have heard *him*.

He began to turn, and instantly Cally pulled her shoulders erect, her eyes not missing that he was critically assessing what she had done, or rather not done, since it always had been her way to leave the kitchen till last.

'You've been hard at it again, I see,' his cold words reached her. He was aware she was there without having to look in her direction.

What a delightful person he is, she thought sourly, and drew his eyes to her at her snappy retort, 'We idle bitches never were known to move like lightning!'

'The remark stung, did it?' His blue eyes looked over her unkempt appearance, and she knew very well, from the way his mouth curled derisively, that he thought she had been asleep upstairs, and had just surfaced on hearing him downstairs. 'A pity it didn't sting sufficiently to get you up off your idle backside.'

'Do all Mexicans have the same endearing personality, or is your charm exclusive?' she queried disdainfully, the colour coming to her cheeks at his insolent comment. Oh, wouldn't she just love to see his face when he saw how the upstairs rooms were taking shape, she thought, near to praying he would take it into his head to do just that.

Her near prayer wasn't answered. 'Tomorrow I shall expect to see an improvement,' he ground out, pushing rudely past her and going to collect the hamper she had barely touched.

'And what punishment should I expect if you don't?' she challenged, moving after him, wonder taking her that she, who had never stood up to her father, should now discover something in her that just refused to back down.

Javier Zarazua had been walking towards the outside door. But at her words, he turned and stood looking at her through slightly narrowed eyes. And Cally knew then, as a prickle of fear rippled along her spine, that he was just the sort of man it would be far wiser to back away from. Was sure of it as bluntly he laid it on the line.

'Because I thought you might need a day or two to get acclimatised, I have overlooked your laziness. You have now been in my country long enough.' And cuttingly, 'It is not in my mind to keep you to decorate this place. Tomorrow, Señorita Shearman, you will get down to work—if I have to stay here all day myself to supervise you.'

Her eyes widened at that, but even while knowing he would be a hard taskmaster, she still wouldn't tell him to take a little walk up those stairs.

'What did I do to deserve you?' she muttered, and went forward as he ignored her and opened the door for them to go through.

'Do you need telling you brought this on yourself by being as avaricious as your brother?'

She threw him a dagger look, and left him to lock up. God, how she hated him! Silently he set the car in motion, and silently they drove on. They had almost reached the house when Cally sent an automatic glance to her wrist to check the time.

'My watch!' she exclaimed, having already decided never to speak to him unless a reply to anything he said couldn't be avoided. She saw him flick a look to her elegant unadorned wrist. 'I left it upstairs back there,' she said, and because she didn't want him doing anything for her, was quick to add, 'It doesn't matter, I can pick it up tomorrow.'

'You thought perhaps I would turn around and go back for it?' he queried sardonically, driving straight on.

'My thoughts about you, *señor*, would turn the air blue if they were given an airing,' she snapped, and was angry suddenly that instead of annoying him as she had hoped, from the brief glance she threw at him she saw that, if anything, her comment had been received with some degree of pleasure.

It was cynical pleasure, she knew that from the way he looked back at her as he drew the car up outside the house and drawled, 'I must be getting to you in some small way if, however blue your thoughts, you are thinking of me, *señorita*.'

Rapidly Cally got out of the car, then realised, as a moment's dizziness seized her, that she still wasn't up to dashing around yet, and clutched on to the door handle, glad he had been concentrating on getting the hamper from the car at just that second. But she still felt the need to have a dig at him, and had that need satisfied as she espied the hamper in his hand.

'And I don't want to have dinner with you tonight either,' she told him arrogantly, 'so please don't ask.'

'I wasn't going to,' he grunted, and marched by her as though she was beneath his notice.

Cally managed by pure will to keep herself from sagging. But once inside her room, the door closed, weak tears spurted to her eyes. It was all she could do to drag herself to the bed and lie down. She had never felt so tired in her life, and his balloon-pricking parting statement left her feeling both mentally and physically exhausted.

Sleep wanting to claim her, she felt too tired to sit up and take off her sandals. Instead she pushed them off one foot against the other, and heard them drop on the floor.

It seemed she had been asleep for only a minute when she heard another sound—a sound in her room. She wanted to keep her eyes closed, wanted to sleep on. But, her brain alerted, she forced her eyelids apart—and then shock to find Javier Zarazua standing there looking down at her had her coming fully awake.

'Wh . . .'

'It is no wonder you are tired, Cally,' he overrode the question that had been in her.

And while her brain was trying to cope with him actually being in her room, he was for once not looking at her in that hard way he usually did, and that—that if her ears weren't deceiving her he had actually called her 'Cally', he was going on to explain his remark:

'Rosa has just been to see me.'

'Rosa?' she replied witlessly, feeling wide awake now, and hoping her brain would catch up soon.

'She was concerned, on unpacking the hamper I returned, that apart from some lemonade, a bite of chicken is all you have had inside you today.'

Cally remembered the lemonade. She had boiled some of it when she couldn't stop a prolonged coughing attack. It had soothed instantly. But the chicken, beautifully cooked though it had been, had tasted like chaff in her mouth.

'I—wasn't hungry,' she said quietly.

Then, her brain at last going into action, she realised she was being far too meek and mild. If she went on this way, she would be back to giving in rather than have a fuss, the way she always had backed away from a row with her father. And she was then asserting herself, was getting some life into that new person she wanted to be.

'And anyway, I don't have to eat your food if I don't want to.'

The hardness in him that had so far been absent came out of hiding at her belligerent tone. 'Is that why you ate nothing yesterday either?' he charged, seeming now to think her lack of appetite had been deliberate, letting her know Rosa had told him about yesterday's hamper too. 'Well, let me tell you, *señorita*,'—so she wasn't Cally any longer?—'that I brought you here to work, to appreciate that you're living in a world where you get nothing for nothing, to know something of good honest toil.'

'For the good of my soul, in other words,' she sat up quickly and jibed, not unaware of the furious glare in his eyes at her manner, although he didn't take her up on what she had said.

'You are *going* to soil your hands—make no mistake about that. So if you're thinking to starve yourself to gain sympathy when you drop from lack of nourishment, then think again. You will eat if I have to spoonfeed you. Got that?' And if she hadn't, 'You know what time I dine,' he threw at her, then flicked an angry glance at her bare wrist and took off his watch and tossed it to the bed. And had one last thing to throw at her before he slammed out. 'Be there!' he barked.

CHAPTER FOUR

CALLY sat exactly where she was for long after he had gone. She glanced at the watch he had more or less thrown at her. It was an expensive one, she saw without much interest, but it told her she had about an hour in which to make up her mind if she was going to join him at his table at eight.

She knew why he intended to make her eat, of course. He wanted his retribution, did Javier Zarazua. He knew full well that if she wasn't fuelling her inner body, she wouldn't have the energy required to experience 'honest toil'. She had discovered that for herself today, for all she had fought against the lethargy in her. But she just didn't feel hungry, had no appetite, and that was plain fact. But that lofty Mexican brute would never accept that, would he?

Just when, in the hate session of him that followed, came the memory of the way he had looked when she had first awakened, she didn't know. But she did not want to remember that there had been no hardness in his eyes then, something akin to warmth if anything. Warmth! she scoffed, hardly. But yet there had been that something there that should have told her there could have been a moment when he was prepared to have a conversation with her without being ready to chop her down to size.

As if she cared, she thought, getting up off the bed and going to stare out of the window. She stood there for long minutes, staring at the magnificent peach tree that grew just outside her room. Then, hating him even more, she left the view and went over to the wardrobe.

Dine with him she would, since it looked as though she would have to. She didn't fancy being spoonfed by him, and he had meant it, the overbearing swine. But if he thought for a minute he wasn't going to have his digestion spoilt because of some mistaken idea that he had bested her, then he could jolly well think again!

After her shower, Cally began to feel better. Under the shower everything he had said about Rolfe had come back to her. And there was a light in her eyes, as she donned one of her two new dresses, that said having been put down all her life, just let him start!

At eight o'clock precisely, Javier Zarazua's wrist watch in her hand, Cally left her room. She knew her new full-length, sleeveless cotton dress suited her, her mirror had told her so. That perhaps her pale cheeks could have done with a hint of colour was the least of her worries.

Expecting to find her dinner companion still in the same foul temper in which she had last seen him, she hid her surprise, the tilt of her chin not ready to be weakened that he greeted her with some semblance of being more agreeable, as he came from an ante-*sala* on hearing her footsteps.

'You would care for an aperitif before your meal, Cally?' he enquired, pocketing the watch she handed him without comment.

So she was Cally again, was she? 'No, thank you, *señor*,' she answered stiffly—and quashed surprise number two, that he didn't rise at her manner, but said smoothly, 'Then permit me to escort you to the dining room. Teresa is waiting to serve.'

Teresa had no smile for her as she ladled soup from an exquisite tureen into her bowl. Cally had hardly expected one, though she had expected she would smile at their employer. But he too was served by an

unsmiling housekeeper. It was then Cally remembered
Javier's remarks about Teresa being a good chaperone.
Perhaps she had seen him go into her bedroom. And
she was suddenly feeling better. Good, it was about
time that arrogant devil got sorted!

Though she was still not hungry, the lift in her spirits
had her raising a spoonful of soup to her mouth. It was
good. She took another spoonful, then saw Teresa
come back into the room with something she had
forgotten and heard Javier say something to her in
Spanish. Then she had her appetite taken away again
that Teresa chose to include in her answer to him a
beaming smile. Manfully she ploughed on. But halfway
through, she laid down her spoon.

'It is not to your liking?'

Trust Hawk-Eye to notice! 'The soup is delicious,' she
answered with polite reserve.

'Then why do you not finish it?'

Oh God, was she going to have this third degree with
every course? 'Because,' she said quietly, trying hard
not to get rattled, 'my appetite is small. I've already
told you that.' And when he continued to look at her,
she felt forced to add, and didn't like him any the better
because of it, 'I—I think perhaps I should leave some
room for what's to follow.'

What followed was the very tenderest of steaks,
served with a side salad. 'I had thought Mexican dishes
would be served with a hundredweight of chili,' left
Cally before it could be held back.

'And I thought,' Javier replied, a light she couldn't
understand in his eyes, 'that since your appetite
apparently needs tempting, it would be better for you to
eat the food you are more accustomed to eating for a
while.'

Astonishment kept her speechless for all of five
seconds. Then she was choking, 'You had Teresa

prepare an English meal especially for me!'

'She was pleased to do it,' he replied carelessly. And, that odd light still there in his eyes, 'I have already complimented her on her way with soup—English style.'

So that was why Teresa had beamed at him. Every employee liked to be complimented on work well done, she thought, though she knew she could wait until the cows came home before he complimented her. Not that *she* wanted his compliments, of course.

Of course she didn't. It was just that . . . She became aware he was observing the inactivity of her knife and fork, and cut a tiny piece from her steak. Teresa had gone to a lot of trouble on her behalf, not to mention Javier's involvement that he had thought to tell his housekeeper to check her recipe books for an English soup. For Teresa's sake, Cally thought, as she popped the small portion of steak into her mouth, she should show willingness.

'Tell me something about your life in England, Cally.' Having supposed it would be a silent meal they shared, Cally found the question unexpected, though she answered civilly enough.

'There's little to tell you, *señor*.'

She looked at him then, and saw from the expression on his face that he wasn't believing her. She discovered then that he must be determined not to let go with his temper, when after taking time out to pour some more wine in her glass, though she had sampled little from it, he merely said:

'Then perhaps you will tell me something of the little there is,' and startling her, he tacked on with throwaway carelessness, 'Call me Javier, by the way. You told me you were not in employment back in England?'

'Er—no—er——'

She was still struggling to realise that he had lowered himself from his lofty height to invite her to call him by his first name, especially since he was reverently referred to as '*El Señor*' by those of his staff she had come into contact with.

'I—er——' She coughed, terrified for a moment that she was going to go off into one of her eye-watering, breath-gasping coughing fits. It didn't happen, and she smiled at him in her relief.

'I lived in a fairly large house with my father,' she said, and wasn't smiling then. For not only was she remembering the querulous man her father was, but at twenty-three, she was suddenly appalled that she had said it all. She had lived in that mausoleum of a house with her father, and that was the sum total of her existence! Javier's next question brought her out of the despair of the thought—when was she ever going to start living her own life?

'You have no mother?'

Thinking of her life back in England had brought an unhappy look to Cally's face. 'No,' she answered, 'she died when I was seven.'

'Your father will be lonely without you?'

With or without Elma Bates, he would not have been lonely, she thought, and wasn't made any happier to realise that she could disappear off the face of the earth, and no one would miss her.

'He's to remarry shortly.'

'Ah, so that is why you decided to leave England,' Javier pounced. 'You do not like his future wife—you are jealous of her.'

Jealous of her! How wrong he was. Elma Bates' timely arrival had given her the chance to escape. She didn't like the woman, admittedly, but it was not jealousy. She would always be grateful to her. It was through her she had her freedom.

She looked across the table at the man who was now sternly studying her, and fate laughed hollowly—what freedom! Until she had worked her fingers to the bone for this tyrant, she was as much his slave as she had ever been her father's.

'I thought you'd already decided on my reason for leaving England. Don't tell me you've changed your mind and now believe I didn't come here to get my avaricious claws on what pickings I could?' Suddenly she was fed up. And, her appetite killed, she stood up.

'You have not finished your meal.' Javier was on his feet too, his height overshadowing her as he barred her way from the room, that hardness back in him at her reminding him of Graciela, her desertion by her avaricious brother, his glance flicking to the half finished steak before he brought his hard eyes back to her face.

'I've eaten all I'm going to,' Cally said stubbornly, and knew then he would have to drag her back to the table before she would sit voluntarily. 'If I eat any more I shall be sick.'

Immediately, his hardness left him. 'You feel ill?' he enquired, a hand coming to take hold of her arm in a supportive gesture. 'I thought earlier how pale you . . .'

'I've never felt better in my life,' she said stiffly, weak tears threatening. 'But I shall feel ten times better if you let go my arm and allow me to go to my room.'

Even as the words left her she knew she stood no chance of him doing as she asked. That was why, when his hand fell to his side, she stood without moving while those blue eyes searched the pallor of her face.

'You don't look . . .'

'Goodnight, *señor*,' Cally said quickly, realising he was letting her go, and, not wanting to hang around to hear what she didn't 'look' in case he took it into his head to change his mind, she went past him.

'Cally!' He called her attention, halted her on the stairs. Weary, not wanting him to see her moist eyes, she kept her back to him. 'We will start out later tomorrow morning,' he told her.

She did not answer, but continued up the stairs. If he was saying he had seen she looked tired and that was his way of suggesting she have a lie-in, then he needn't have bothered. She wanted no favours from him. She needed to get to work, needed to get that air fare earned so that she could go home.

Though, as she flopped into bed not many minutes later, Cally couldn't help wondering where she was going to get the energy to hang those heavy curtains up tomorrow.

A coughing fit woke her in the night, had her breathless and gasping. Her cough should have cleared by now, she thought, as her breathing steadied. Though since she had been shut up in that house for most of the time, there had been very little chance for the sun the doctor had ordered to get through to her.

Exhausted by her coughing bout, she lay down—and immediately began coughing again. Feeling spent, she sat up, bathed in perspiration, and threw back the covers, knowing only an urgent desire for some warm lemonade—it had stopped her coughing before. She would clear up after her and Teresa would never know she had been in her kitchen.

Pulling on her cotton robe over the short cotton nightdress she wore, Cally leaned weakly against the door, wanting a break in her coughing before she opened it.

Her hand covering her mouth, she made it to the kitchen, where she put on the light and closed the door. But before she could start looking for lemons, she just had to sit down. She felt dreadful, spent, and was glad no one could see her, since she had a fair idea she must be looking as ghastly as she felt. Pride demanded that Javier Zarazua knew nothing of this. He would only say she had deliberately brought it on herself by not eating, she thought, her head starting to swim.

She made herself leave her chair, knowing she needed all the sleep she could get if she was going to be fit enough to work tomorrow. But she got no farther than a few steps when the door behind her opened, and too quickly she swung round.

Through swirling mists of dizziness she saw the man she didn't want to know about her night-time excursion, though she could not make out his expression as he surveyed her damp tousled hair and pasty complexion. But the *'Dios!'* that left him, as she put all her will to staying upright, gave her some idea that he wasn't very pleased with her.

He didn't waste time in commenting on her appearance. And hate him as she did, Cally found enormous relief as she started to sway when in a stride he was up to her, his brick wall body there for her to lean on.

Weakly she clutched at him, resting her body against his until the world righted itself. But knowing she was no longer threatened by a faint, the effort to move seemed too much, and she stayed there against him as she forgot she didn't want him to know, and gaspingly explained:

'I came down—for some—warm lemonade. I—I can't stop—c-coughing.'

The last word was said in a splutter, and she was off again, being racked by that dry hard cough. She couldn't even apologise as he held her to him, she had need of all her breath.

Her body was soaked in perspiration when her coughing was done, the dampness saturating her clothes as Javier held her. Then the shoulder she had returned to weakly lean against moved, and he was pulling back to see into her exhausted face. And as she looked back, and said a husky, 'I'm sorry,' she saw there was no hardness in him.

Cally thought she must be near to being delirious when she saw the corners of his mouth pick up in what looked to be a smile, grim though it appeared. A smile for her! Then those strong hands were moving her into a chair.

'Sit there for a moment, Cally,' he said, so mildly, so kindly, she was certain she was either dreaming or definitely delirious. Never had he spoken to her that way.

She sat where he placed her, simply because she hadn't the energy to do anything else, her tired eyes watching the efficient way he dealt with lemons, sugar and water, the way he found a saucepan. And lightheaded though she knew herself to be, she just knew she wasn't imagining that the brute she had known was making a warm lemon drink for her.

He set the saucepan on a low light, then came back to look at her, his hand coming to her damp forehead, and she saw when she looked up, her grey-green eyes wide, that his face was looking serious as he took his hand away.

'I won't be long,' he said, and gave her a smile of such charm, she just couldn't believe it.

He wasn't long. But Cally was coughing again when he returned, and he lost no time in checking the temperature of the contents in the saucepan, or pouring it into a beaker and bringing it over to her.

'Sip it slowly,' he advised, when she had recovered sufficiently to do as he requested.

Relief was instant. It was like syrup to her ragged throat. 'Thank you,' she whispered, and took another sip of the simple yet magical concoction.

She peered into the saucepan he had placed down on the kitchen table, and saw there was some left. And being nervous of having another attack when back in her room, she said:

'I'm all right now. But could I take some of that to my room?'

'I'll put some in a flask . . .'

'Oh, there's no need,' she said quickly, only now conscious that he too was in a robe, that he must have heard her even though she had tried to stifle her cough when coming downstairs. Conscious that she had broken his night's sleep, she was conscious also that where, if she had judged him accurately, he should be livid at the pest she was being—her father would have been—Javier didn't seem to be put out at all.

For answer, he smiled, and since he made no move to fetch the flask he had spoken of, she thought he had taken her at her word. Reaching for the saucepan, she would have tipped the liquid into her beaker to take back with her.

'Leave it there, Cally.' She looked up. 'I'll bring it up to you.'

About to tell him again that there was no need, that she could carry it, she changed her mind. She still felt shaky. The lemon and sugar substance would dry sticky on the costly-looking carpeting if it slopped over while she climbed the stairs. And suddenly she knew she was going to need every scrap of her strength to make it to the top of those stairs. She stood up, her legs weak.

'You are ready to return to your bed?'

'Yes,' she replied. And because she was feeling so lightheaded, when she said, 'Thank you,' she added, 'Javier.'

He really was taking all this very well, she thought, when his answer to her was nothing but a pleased kind of smile. And then topping everything he had so far done for her, just when she was thinking she had better get moving and try to make each step look as though she wasn't anywhere near as rocky as she felt, before she could take more than two tottery steps, she felt his arms come round her. And the next thing she knew, he was carrying her back to bed, his tone casual as he remarked:

'It will be quicker this way, I think.'

Bemused, she thought perhaps illness brought out the best in the man. Though of course she wasn't ill—just feeling the effects of the altitude and that annoying cough which was taking its time in leaving.

She was drowsy when he opened the door to her room, her head against his chest because it was the most convenient resting place.

Gently he placed her on the bed. 'Can you manage by yourself?' he enquired, his hands already at the tie of her robe.

Drowsiness departed. 'Oh yes,' she said brightly, something inside her doing a quick flip. 'I'm quite all right now.'

'I'm sure you are,' he said. But he didn't sound at all as though he believed it.

'I am,' she said. And because he was this new Javier Zarazua, the one who smiled, her customary reserve, perhaps because he had been so nice, melted, and she in turn smiled at him.

And if her smile for him had shaken him as much as his smile for her had shaken her, then after staring at her mouth for a serious second, Javier suddenly straightened from the bed.

'I'll go and get that lemonade,' he said. And she knew from the gruff way he said it that his pleasantness was at an end.

She was just thinking she would wait only until he had returned with the lemonade and had gone and then she would exchange her damp nightdress for a dry one, when car headlights sweeping the drive, hitting her window, sent the idea from her head. Who on earth would be calling at this time of night? Or had she imagined that, the same way she had imagined Javier had looked pleased when she had called him by his first name?

Cally was to discover that it wasn't her imagination, that there was a night-time visitor to the ranch. For when Javier returned, a vacuum flash and a fresh beaker in his hands, he was not alone.

'This is my friend Dr Tenreiro,' Javier explained his male companion who came into the room behind him, before she could get panicky.

'Doctor? I don't . . .'

'Need a doctor?' Javier finished for her. Then, looking ready to get tough, 'I have discovered in you, Cally Shearman, a determination not to give in. Permit me, as the man who has taken charge of you while you are in my country, to know what is best for you.'

There was no arguing with that tone, though had she been feeling more herself, Cally thought she would have tried. As it was she was left feeling stupid when the doctor, looking more like a Mexican to her way of thinking, with his dark hair and dark eyes, approached the bed and came to look at her. But her attention was taken from Dr Tenreiro as she heard Javier say:

'I will get Teresa.'

'No!' sprang from her, causing the attention of both men to focus on her.

'I wish Ramon to examine you,' Javier told her tautly, letting her know his word was law. But her lips had set in a stubborn line.

'I have caused enough upset,' she said woodenly. 'First you out of bed in the middle of the night, now Dr Tenreiro.' He must have phoned him when he had briefly left the kitchen, she saw. 'I will not have Teresa's night's rest disturbed.'

His eyes flicked her mutinous face. 'You have no choice in the matter,' he said abruptly. Then as she watched, she saw that devil in him again. 'Though of course, I can always stay to chaperone if . . .'

'No!' It came out sharply as she cringed from the very idea. And she began hating Javier Zarazua again when, with that lofty look back with him, he went to rouse Teresa from her bed.

The doctor, whose English, though not as fluent as his friend's, was good, was seated beside the bed, having cleverly extracted from Cally all there was to be learned about the strong virus strain that had flattened her in England, and had left her with a cough she had despaired of losing, when Teresa came hurrying into the room.

It all seemed a great deal of fuss over nothing, Cally thought, when in minutes, it seemed, the doctor had examined her and Teresa had helped her into a fresh nightie. All that was wrong with her was a cough that wouldn't clear up. She wished they would all go away and leave her in peace—she felt so tired, she could sleep the clock round.

So tired was she that within minutes of Teresa and the doctor leaving, she was fast asleep. She had no idea that Javier Zarazua had spent those minutes in conversation with the doctor. No idea that Javier had returned to her room and stood looking down at her pale worn out face, her fair wavy hair spread over her pillow. For one minute more Javier stood watching her in sleep, then he put out the small table lamp beside her bed, and he too left the room.

It all seemed like a dream when Cally awakened the next morning. She was still uncertain that it had not in fact been a dream. That was until she looked at the nightdress she was wearing, and then saw the vacuum flask.

Had she really called Javier Zarazua by his first name last night? The realisation that she had saw her getting out of bed. Beneath the shower she wished she had some idea of the time. She felt nowhere up to being supervised at her work. Then, remembering the way Javier's attitude had hardened when she had said she didn't want Teresa disturbed, she reckoned he would soon be breathing down her neck if she didn't get a move on.

She almost didn't put her robe back on after coming from under the shower. It would have saved time if she'd just gone quickly into the bedroom to dress. But the repressions of her childhood had her pulling into it. And when she stepped into her bedroom, she was glad she had.

Javier Zarazua was there. He was standing, leaning idly against the dressing table, his eyes watching her, as her face pale still, she hurried into the room.

'I'm late, I know,' she said before he could get a word in. And, searching for an excuse, uncomfortable with him there as she took out the jeans and sleeveless shirt she intended to don the minute he had gone, 'You know my watch is . . .' His voice, mild, but firm had her breaking off.

'Just what the hell do you think you're doing?'

Startled, she looked at him. 'Why, getting ready to go to work, of course,' she said. 'There was no need to come and get me. I was on my . . .'

'Am I such a brute?' His roughly asked question stopped her.

She remembered last night, his kindness, the way he had carried her to her room, and the gentle way he had laid her on her bed. It weakened her. But she couldn't afford to be weak where he was concerned. He'd be snapping and snarling at her any minute now, and she knew she'd regret it if she let him see her weakness.

'In a word—yes,' she told him bluntly. 'You are a brute. And—and if you'll kindly take yourself off, I'll get dressed and be ready to go . . .'

'The only place you're going, young Cally,' he interrupted, 'is back to bed.'

Oh, how the idea appealed! 'I . . .' she began, and wanted dreadfully to give in to that idea. Then thoughts of never getting out from this man's roof were on her. 'What—and give you the satisfaction of saying I'd made myself ill on purpose so I could be waited on? Not likely!'

'I didn't know then you had been ill. Why didn't you tell me?'

'Good grief, it was only 'flu,' she protested, starting to feel used up already, although she hadn't been out of bed long, and hadn't yet done a stroke.

'But a particularly powerful virus, I believe. Ramon Tenreiro recognised it as such from what I told him about your cough and from what you yourself told him.'

Cally would like to have sat down. But since pride wouldn't have her showing him any more weakness than Javier had already seen, then the best thing she could do was to terminate this conversation and get rid of him.

'Well, there's nothing wrong with me that a spot of sunshine won't cure—my doctor in England told me that, so . . .'

'So you've certainly come to the right place,' he finished for her, which hadn't been what she had been about to say at all. 'And since you're rocking on your feet but won't admit it, I think, for a start, we'll get you into bed.'

'*We'll* do no such thing,' she said hotly—and then

felt ready to collapse when Javier said no more, but looked as though he had done trying to reason with her and came over to her, grasping her by the arms, and looking ready to shake some sense into her.

'Don't be rough with me!' Despising her own weakness as she did, Cally couldn't hold back the words of fear. She was feeling weepy again and was dreadfully afraid tears would fall if he shook her.

'I don't want to be rough with you,' he said, his voice quiet suddenly. Then he was pulling her to sit on the bed, sitting there beside her, as he revealed, 'Ramon had told me you require complete rest. Give in, Cally, you know damn well you're not up to work.'

She wanted to argue that she was, saw he read in her eyes she wasn't ready to admit defeat, and then she saw again that smile she had thought a figment of her imagination.

'Give in,' he urged. 'You know I'm not going to take you to that house again.' And looking into his eyes Cally felt the most peculiar feelings start up inside her when he said softly, 'Are you going to make me eat dirt that I was a swine to you for not doing work I should have seen you were feeling too ill to do yesterday and the day before?'

'But I . . .'

'Are you, Cally?' he pressed, when she was certain nobody could ever make him eat dirt.

'No,' she said, and swallowed, so mesmerised by the charm of him that when, gently, his mouth met hers in a fleeting kiss, she had given in completely, and didn't have a thought in her head to back away.

But the thought was in his head, for after drawing away he was looking deeply into her grey-green eyes, scanning her face, and standing up to ask quietly:

'Where do you keep your nightwear?'

And Cally, still stunned that he had kissed her, told
him. She was still sitting there when he returned from
the bathroom, having taken her nightdress from the peg
she had left it on.

She must have been stupefied, she thought afterwards.
For she had no resistance to make when he popped her
nightdress over her head and then, just as though he
had performed the same service every day of his life, he
whipped away her robe, shocking her out of her
mesmeric state as she saw, as he must in the second
before her nightdress was brought down to cover the
rest of her, her uptilted pink-tipped breasts, her hips
and thighs.

Colour flamed through her so she thought she would
roast alive, flaming colour he couldn't miss seeing even
if he was near-sighted, which she was positive he wasn't.

And momentarily, she was back to hating him, even
though she was hearing him laugh for the first time.
Laugh joyfully, before he put his laughter from him,
and teased:

'Why, Cally Shearman, shame on you! I do believe
I'm the first man outside the medical profession to
catch a glimpse of your beautiful body!' And while she
was still crimson with mortification—mortification
added to the fact that he thought she must be as old-
fashioned as Methuselah's buck goat, he was endorsing
that he thought her far from womanly, by saying:

'Come now, *niña*—into bed. Teresa is waiting to boil
you a British four-minute egg with toasted soldiers.'

CHAPTER FIVE

CALLY slept for most of that day. But there were moments of waking, moments when she would liked to have got her cottonwool thoughts together, to wonder about that kiss she had shared with Javier Zarazua. For shared it had been. And brief though it had been, it had been a kiss from a man to a woman—regardless that he had afterwards treated her as a child.

But there was no time for her to wonder why she hadn't pushed him away, why she should find his kiss not unpleasant when she had thought she hated him so much. Because as if they had been hovering just waiting for her to open her eyes, each time she did so, she found either Teresa or Rosa in attendance.

When she surfaced from sleep and discovered she just wasn't sleepy any more, that she felt the return of some of her former energy, it was about to grow dusk outside. And for once there was no Rosa or Teresa there.

She contemplated getting up. She had never been so fussed over in her life, and considered she had put everyone to more than enough trouble. She turned her head and saw a different vacuum flask reposing on the bedside table, indicating that either Teresa or Rosa had been in and brought her some fresh lemonade should she require it.

They really shouldn't be waiting on her like this, she thought, and would then have got out of bed, but remembrance of that light kiss she had shared with Javier that morning came hurtling in, and with it, remembrance of the way he had matter-of-factly popped her into her nightie. And she knew then, as pink warmed her cheeks, that she just wasn't up to facing him across the dinner table. She just wasn't ready to see him again yet.

Then she discovered, as she heard the tread of masculine footsteps along the landing, that Javier Zarazua wasn't the sort of man who waited for an invitation if it was in his mind to come calling.

Her eyes searched frantically for her hairbrush, a vanity unknown to her before, as she heard those footsteps halt outside her door. And she had no time to brush the tumbled mass of waves into any sort of order around her shoulders either. For without his bothering to knock, the door swung inwards and the tall Mexican was approaching the bed, his blue eyes not missing a thing about her appearance, the look on his face grim though Cally was sure since she was feeling so much better, she must look it.

'You lied to me,' he said without preamble, his words as harsh as the look on his face. And, not waiting for her to deny the charge, not taking his eyes from her, he put his hand in his pocket and threw her watch down on the coverlet. Her eyes went from the watch she had last seen when she had left it in one of those upstairs rooms in the overseer's house, and up to his face.

'I thought you might be needing that,' he said, his thoughtfulness in going to fetch it for her surprising her, though this, she saw, just wasn't the moment to thank him—he was *fuming*! 'You must have slogged your guts out to have got so much done,' he tossed at her harshly. 'No wonder you were flattened!' And as if he couldn't bear to look at her, he went to the window to stare morosely out.

Cally realised she should say something. But by the look of him his temper was riding on a short fuse. She

was used to placating her father, and was on the point
of trying the same with her grim-looking employer,
when the thought came—why should she? So—he
didn't like it that because of his opinion of her she had
rendered herself into a state of exhaustion. So what?

But, torn between the person she had been, and the
person she wanted to be, Cally could see she would
never get away from her old ways if she fell at the first
hurdle. Why should she think of trying to placate him
after the dreadful things he had said in the past—why
should she be afraid of his anger anyway?

'When did I lie to you?' she challenged his blue-
shirted back, and had to hang on hard to the new-
found Cally when he swung from the window and came
to tower over her.

'By implication you lied. You could have told me any
time—yesterday, the day before, that you had decided
to clean the house from the top down.' His jaw jutted as
he recalled, 'Not one word did you say when I called
you an idle bitch. It stung you, I know it did, but still
you didn't say a word.'

'I was expecting you to take a tour round to see what
I'd done,' she said, then realised her old habit of being
placatory was hard a-dying. 'Anyway,' she sloughed off
the old habit, 'it serves you right, you shouldn't have
assumed . . .'

'It wasn't *me* who suffered,' he blazed, looking very
much as though he was adding 'stupid' to the rest of the
names he reserved for her.

'So I suffered,' she said airily. 'And now I'm well
again. So we needn't argue the point any more.' And,
greatly daring since she could see she hadn't improved
his temper any by her haughty attitude, 'Close the door
on your way out.'

The fire that flamed in his eyes at her insolence had her
wishing she had held down that last bit. 'Why, you . . .'

he muttered, enraged, looking ready to throttle her.

Ready to start yelling, I'm sorry, sorry, sorry! Cally discovered, even though death looked imminent, that the determination Javier had discovered in her was refusing to leave and make way for the urgent apology. And then she was glad she hadn't apologised, because he had somehow gained control of his temper, though not, she thought, because he had observed the way her face had paled at the aggression in him.

'You are right,' he said, and she knew if physically he wasn't going to set about her, then she just had to be in for a lashing from his tongue. 'I was wrong to assume you were lazy. You're prepared to work hard to get what you want, aren't you, my lovely?'

'Get what I want?' She ignored the 'my lovely' part, there was no sincerity in it.

'Are you not, after all, seeking my good opinion of you? Did you not labour over washing and ironing those curtains when you were ready to drop, with the sole intention of appearing lost and appealing when I found you exhausted last night?'

Open-mouthed, she stared at him. 'You think . . .' she gasped.

'That you have realised there are far greater pickings to be had here than the leavings your brother would ever have allowed you?' He shrugged, his insolence far outweighing any of hers. 'I'll leave you to prove me wrong, Cally Shearman,' he said with false charm, and left *her* fuming, as casually he strode out.

Cally was up early the following morning, fuming again that she didn't care a fig for Javier Zarazua's opinion of her, as last night after he had gone she had fumed. And it wasn't her intention to prove anything to him as she made her way downstairs. All that was in her mind, even if she was aware that she did not yet feel quite up to the mark, was that the sooner she got to work, the sooner her air fare would be earned and she could be away from his cynical baiting.

He came out into the hall just as she reached the bottom of the stairs. Many of the rooms had no doors, but archways, to let the air circulate. But whether he had heard her she neither knew nor cared. Though it was Javier who was first to speak, his voice sardonic as his eyes flicked over her shirt and jean-clad figure.

'And just what quaint notion do we have in our head this morning?' he asked, looking arrogantly down at her, making her wish she had stayed two stairs up.

'At the risk of you thinking I'm out to prove anything to you,' she shot back, 'I've decided to work today.'

She didn't miss the look of exasperation that came momentarily to him. But it was brief, and didn't last. For suddenly his look became speculative, and all at once that devil was there in his eyes.

'My assumptions—in your case—have been known to have been wrong before,' he drawled, his eyes raking over her breasts, her hips. 'Am I to assume that you were not embarrassed this time yesterday? Did my eyes deceive me in that you did not wear a colour a lobster would have envied, when I dressed you for bed?'

'Wh-what do you mean!' she asked, scandalised. He couldn't mean what it sounded as though he was meaning?

She saw the devilish light go from him, as with his expression hard, his tone saying he meant every word, he clipped sharply:

'I'll give you ten seconds to get back upstairs. If you haven't moved by then I shall carry you to your room, and shall personally put you back into bed.'

'You—wouldn't!' Even as she said it, she knew that he damn well would.

'Four,' he counted, 'five.'

'You swine! You Mexican swine!' she shouted furiously.

'Eight, nine . . .'

Half way back up the stairs, Cally heard his laugh behind her, and wished violently that she had something in her hand to throw at him. Mexican men, so she had heard, expected their women to be submissive, but she wasn't his woman, and she didn't intend to be submissive either. She had been submissive all her life. Trust her to choose Mexico of all places to begin her liberation!

From her bedroom she saw him leave—not by car, as other mornings had been his mode of transport. It was the sound of horse's hooves that had her at the window, and it was to see him ride away on a magnificent black stallion. I hope it throws him, she thought mutinously. But there was little chance of that, she saw, for both horse and rider moved as one.

Anticipating that he had gone out on the range, and would be out all day, Cally determined not to be subdued by him and obediently return to her bed, and went down to the kitchen to offer assistance the moment the sound of horse's hooves had died away.

By sweeping actions, washing up actions, dusting, polishing, she thought she had got through to Teresa that she wanted some work. She was sure she had got through to her, and her heart lifted as Teresa indicated that she should follow her.

But her spirits dipped when after following her along the hall and through a lounge area, Teresa took her out on to a patio where she signed that Cally should lie down on the sun-lounger and rest. The many times the words *'El Señor'* were interspered in the flow of Spanish, a good enough indication that the *Señor* had ordered that she must not do a hand's turn all day.

Not wanting to upset Teresa, who had been an angel
to her yesterday, albeit an unsmiling one, resignedly
Cally stretched out on the lounger. And then,
unbelievably, she did catch a glimpse of Teresa's gold-
rimmed toothy smile as she nodded approvingly, then
went back to her labours.

For an hour Cally lay there, and at first her thoughts
held nothing but mutiny. But the breathtaking view to
be seen from the patio, high ranges of hills, varying
shades of green, surmounted by a clear blue sky, simply
left no place for the sourness of her thoughts. Nearby
was a swimming pool, its waters inviting, although she
wasn't a brilliant swimmer. Beyond the pool were green
lawns, flowers, irises of every colour, roses, marguer-
ites—peace washed over her.

Her eyes left the beautiful flower beds, her attention
attracted by a man doing some digging. He was a man
nearing fifty, a corpulent man. He had seen her too,
and was near enough to see her had she smiled. But
something in the way he looked at her had her holding
back on that smile. Something about the man made her
feel uncomfortable, something she couldn't quite put
her finger on. It decided her that today at any rate she
wasn't going to try out her basic swimming strokes in
that pool.

On the point of deciding that she wasn't enjoying
lying there any more, not certain at which point she had
begun to enjoy it, she saw Rosa come out with a tray of
coffee. The, 'I didn't know you had arrived,' that came
from Cally was received blankly by the pretty girl,
though she smiled and Cally smiled back.

Then she saw Rosa had seen the gardener too, and
realised he must be quite harmless, when Rosa called,
'Manuel—café!'

Cally sipped her coffee and with Manuel no longer
there, began to relax. She even began to feel happy

when the tiny tot Rosalinda trotted out to her and, her shyness overcome, regardless that Cally couldn't understand or make herself understood to the delightful child, she began jabbering away ten to the dozen, the word *'fiesta'* coming up time and time again.

Rosa, loving the child, as was apparent, did not leave it for very long before she came out looking for her. And amazing though Cally found it, knowing barely any Spanish, when she said *'Fiesta'* and signed that Rosalinda had been talking about one such, she learned that the child was to have a birthday party soon, Rosa holding up four fingers to indicate that the little mite would be four years old any day now.

Strange though it was, for she had done nothing all day, by the time eight o'clock approached Cally was getting to feel hungry. She had eaten a light lunch, nothing at all like the heavy meal she had witnessed Arturo and Manuel eating in the kitchen when she had, amidst protests, carried her used dishes to the kitchen. Though she had learned then that Manuel was a sort of odd job man about the place.

Thinking it wiser not to sit out in the sun too long, she had gone for a walk during the afternoon. There were many outbuildings and paddocks to be seen, several men, dark-haired and brown-eyed, unlike their employer, all without exception, or so it seemed, wearing a straw hat, not the sombrero type Cally had imagined, but with a brim of about three inches, with a short coloured tassel at the back that she thought must be to distract flies.

Would Javier expect her to have a dinner tray in her room? she pondered. He had sent her there without having to stir himself too much after all, hadn't he? Mutiny returned, but she quelled it. She wanted to have a talk with him, and there was no sense getting off on the wrong foot.

She dressed in the long-skirted dress she had worn the only other time she had dined with him, reasoning that Teresa would have given him a full account of her being up and about. And anyway, since he had assumed she had made herself ill on purpose, wasn't it natural, with him being so quick with his assumptions, that he would think she would expect to have Teresa wait on her in her room?

Not wanting him to come and order her downstairs, at a quarter to eight Cally presented herself in the ante-*sala*. It was there she found Javier pouring himself what looked like a Scotch.

'You don't favour the Tequila, I see?' she got in first, showing him she was ready to be polite, and not giving a damn which way his assumptions went if he was trying to make anything from it.

'Occasionally,' he answered, taking her appearance downstairs for granted as his eyes went over her. 'You are looking improved,' he stated, not expecting a reply. 'What would you like to drink?'

'May I have a sherry?'

He motioned her to a chair, while he stood at the carved wood bar and poured it for her. Then bringing his glass with him, he set her sherry on the low table before her and took the seat opposite while she watched, noting how well he looked in his lightweight tailored suit, and that his hair looked darker—probably still damp from his shower, she thought.

She was determined to keep it casual, she wanted him to keep his aggression to himself until she had the answer to something that had been with her all day, but she was slightly aghast to hear herself say:

'Your hair is lighter than other Mexicans I've seen.' Then felt dreadful, as quickly she added, 'I'm sorry, I didn't mean to be impolite.'

She hadn't offended him, she saw, and she began to

feel easier when he unbent sufficiently to enquire, his manner relaxed, 'My hair colour puzzles you?'

'Er—yes,' she confessed, and owned, 'I've never seen a Mexican with blue eyes either.'

'There are many such in the north,' he enlightened her, taking a swallow of his drink. 'It is generally believed we take our colouring from French antecedents rather than Spanish.'

He then went on to relate how the Emperor Maximilian had received support from the French, some of whom had stayed behind and married local girls. He had a witty turn of phrase and soon had Cally's mind going from the question she really wanted to ask him, as she asked instead if because of his ancestors he had troubled to learn French.

'Oui,' he replied, and that French 'Yes' had her smiling, because somehow he had made it sound comical. She was aware that his eyes stayed on her, and didn't understand why, until he said, 'You become beautiful when you smile, Cally, you should do it more often.'

That took her aback. It had to be a compliment, but he had made it sound so matter-of-fact, perhaps he hadn't intended it as a compliment. And anyway, she thought, trying to get a grip on herself that she should forget herself so far as to be pleased that he thought she could sometimes look beautiful, what, to begin with, had she got to smile about?

'You—speak English fluently too,' she said, and saw it was his turn to curve his mouth that she was wasting no time in getting him off the subject of her smile.

'I had a few years' education in the United States,' he revealed. And glancing at her sherry glass, which she had no recollection of emptying, he terminated the conversation by saying, 'I see you have finished your drink. Would you like another, or shall we have dinner?'

'Dinner, I think,' she replied, leaving her chair, of the opinion that two sherries would have her singing 'Nellie Dean.'

'A thought has amused you?'

'I was—er—just thinking—I hadn't—er—better have any more to drink. I'm not used to it.'

Not wanting to see if he greeted that remark with scepticism or not, she preceded him to the dining room. But when he poured her a glass of wine to complement her meal, he did observe:

'It is only a light wine. Quite innocuous, I assure you.'

Cally left it until nearly the end of the meal to ask the question that had been burning on her tongue. Unbelievably, not one hard or heated word had passed across the table. And if what she had to ask him took the edge away from her being fully relaxed, there was nothing but a casual ease in his manner, as he looked up, arrested, when she said:

'Javier . . .'

Or *was* his manner so casual? she wondered, having got his attention. There was an alert look at the back of those blue eyes. But he couldn't know she had been careful not to cross him for the past hour because she wanted him to do her one big favour, could he? Of course he couldn't, she denied. And since he was silently waiting for her to spit out why she had called his attention to her, the sooner she got it out into the open the better.

'I was wondering——' she began, and was already faltering, embarrassment flooding her at what she just had to ask.

'I'm listening,' he prompted.

'Well, I—well, I don't seem to be making much of a job—at working for my air fare.'

'Strange,' he replied, a smile around his mouth, but

nowhere near his eyes, she noticed. 'It is my opinion that you have so far done exceedingly well in the work I set you.'

Cally had the oddest feeling that he was being difficult on purpose. He wasn't so thick—wasn't thick at all, she knew that. But having made mention of her air fare, she was sure he just knew what she wanted to ask—and was deliberately making her come right out with it, when he could just as easily have helped her out a little.

'Well, I don't think I have,' she said. And unable to look at him to see that pretence of a curve to his mouth straighten if she didn't word it right, she went on, 'So I was wondering—if—er—if . . .'

She had to flick a glance at him, and was annoyed that his expression hadn't changed, annoyed that he was content to sit there and let her try and get it together. Her annoyance sent tact to the four winds, had her bringing out what she wanted to ask flatly, with no sign about her that it would be the biggest favour she had ever asked of anyone.

'Will you lend me my air fare to England?'

The words out, she concealed that she was waiting breathless for his reply, and held her head proudly, ready for his refusal if that was to be his answer.

'Lend?' he queried after a pause that seemed to her to go on for ever, and as she suspected, with that curve gone from his mouth.

But she saw some encouragement there, in that he hadn't given her a flat refusal, had he? And she was in quickly, her seeming arrogance gone, as she told him:

'I'll pay you back, every penny. And I know it wouldn't be running you short to give me that money. I had a look round this aft . . .'

'So——' Aggression she had hoped would stay absent was starting to rear. 'You have been poking around, have judged for yourself the extent of my riches.'

'No—No, it wasn't like that. I went for a walk, yes, but not to—poke around, as you call it.'

Damn him, this was going all wrong. Far from even getting started on making him see her point of view, all she had succeeded in doing was confirm that she was as money-oriented as he believed Rolfe was.

She didn't have any idea how she was going to get him to see how sincere she was, but yet she had to. Had to sit there and take all he threw, because it was just too important to her, that she couldn't yell at him as she wanted, 'Forget it', and go to her room. She had to get out of here—and only through him was that going to be achieved. But before she could get her words into any sort of order, Javier was mocking:

'You sound very eager to leave—are you saying you don't like it here?'

His sarcasm she could do without. 'Your home is in a very beautiful spot,' she said, trying to keep cool, though speaking the truth. 'And—and if the circumstances had been—different, I think I would be delighted at the opportunity to—spend some time here. But . . .'

'But you have realised I am no pushover for your beautiful soulful eyes?'

'Damn you!' she snapped, fury jetting to the surface, her tact in smithereens at being accused of being a gold-digger yet again.

His answer was a cool smile at having wrecked her front. But there was that in his eyes that showed a glimmer of—was it admiration that eyes he had just called beautiful were spitting fire at him? Or was it satisfaction that he had succeeded so easily in removing her cloak of reserved cool?

'You said you would pay me back—er—should I

accede to your request for your air fare?' Calmly he
took the heat out of her by going back to that all-
important subject. And having been near to throwing
the water jug at him, Cally took a deep and steadying
breath that, accusations out of the way, it looked as
though he was ready to talk business.

'Yes, of course,' she said, still feeling a shade uptight
that he thought she would ask any man for money
without any intention of repayment. 'It would only be a
loan.'

'May I ask how you intend to repay me?' It was a
natural question, a question any business man would
ask, she thought, begining to feel better. 'From my
understanding, your father must be as impecunious as
yourself, otherwise you would have cabled him for your
air fare from the hotel in Querétaro.'

She hadn't even thought to do that, purely she knew
because even her subconscious was aware it would have
been a waste of precious pesos to cable her father.

'My father is not without means,' she said, pride
forcing the words between her lips, memory of the
money he would get from the sale of the house there.
Even if the proceeds were split between him and Elma
Bates, which was only fair, that still left him with a tidy
sum.

'But he is not disposed to send any of his means your
way?'

'He paid my fare out,' Cally said shortly, wondering
why on earth he was dragging her father into this—and
had her breath caught sharply in her throat as, harshly,
Javier bit at her:

'For a man who appears as tight-fisted as he does,
that sounds as though he was willing to pay to get rid
of you.' And on the heels of that, the straightforward
question, '*Was* he glad to be rid of you?'

That the question caused her hurt made Cally aware

she must have some regard for her father after all.
'There was no place for me in his home with his new
wife,' she said quietly—and knew it wasn't because
Javier thought he might have hurt her that his voice had
softened when he asked:

'Does your father not love you?'

It was her turn to be mocking. She didn't want him
to see that the inner knowledge of the answer to that
question hurt too.

'He never said.'

'When love is there it doesn't have to be said.
Knowledge is instinctive.'

Cally was hating him again. 'Then I think I can take
it my father had little regard for me,' she said stonily.
And, fed up with him and this conversation when Javier
looked steadily at her without any answering comment,
'And I would rather not discuss my father or his lack of
affection for me, if you don't mind.'

'Very well. We will return to how you propose to
repay any loan I might consider making you.'

'I'd get a job,' she said without hesitation, her spirits
starting to rise again. 'Once back in England I would
find work.'

'Doing what? If you were telling me the truth, you
said you had never worked before.'

'I . . .' Stumped, she hadn't got as far as thinking
what work she was going to do. Her first essential once
her plane had landed was to find somewhere to live.
'I've never been in paid employment, I'll admit, but I
was my father's housekeeper. I kept the house
immaculate too,' she didn't mind admitting. Javier had
to see she wasn't afraid of work.

'I don't doubt it.' He sounded sincere, and she knew
then he was remembering the work she had put in at the
overseer's house.

'I wouldn't ask you,' she went on, feeling a whole

heap better since it looked as though she had his trust that she wouldn't let any employer down, 'only since I can't find Rolfe, I . . .'

She had blown it. She knew she had the moment Rolfe's name had left her. Any semblance of cordiality in Javier went from him, and she knew all he was remembering then was the hurt one member of his family had suffered from the hands of a member of her family. She saw it there in the sudden thrust of his jaw, saw that his hatred of Rolfe and all he had done was too much to be contained, as he pushed his chair back and stood, civility at an end.

'Your appetite is improving,' he said stiffly, thereby letting her know he had been observing her while she ate. And her hate rose to the surface again as she realised that had been the only reason for his easy way throughout the meal—as if he knew had hostility been there she would have had small appetite. 'But since the meal is now over, I must ask you to excuse me. I have papers to attend to.'

'But—but what about my air fare?' Rising to her feet, she moved forward, reaching the door at the same time as him. She hadn't sat all through that only to have the door slammed on her hopes.

'Your air fare?' Her arrogance was a non-starter beside his as he looked down at her. 'You have suggested you will work for it, and so you will—but not in your own country.'

'I'm to stay—here?' She couldn't believe it. She had pinned all her hopes . . .

'For some time, I think.' His look that had been ruthless, hardened to granite as he rapped, 'That is unless you intend quickly to follow your brother's example.' So his thoughts were still on Rolfe.

'I don't—understand you.'

'No——? Your brother thought he had found himself a wealthy woman, did he not?'

'You think . . .' Cally swallowed, choking on what she saw he did think. 'You think I'd make a—play for you to get my air fare without working for it!'

'I don't recall you objecting too strongly when I kissed you yesterday,' he told her loftily, and as the colour surged into her face that he too had taken note there hadn't been a protest about her, he added, 'In fact, from my recollections, you didn't object at all.'

Whether it was his overbearing arrogance that riled her then, or if it was the shame in her soul that he was speaking the truth that got to her, she didn't know. But that right hand that had positively itched many times to have a go at him would no longer be quieted, and before she knew it, it had chosen just that moment to arc through the air.

She cut him squarely across the face, hardly aware of what she had done, her hand seeming to act of its own volition.

'While we're on the subject of recollections,' she spat into the tense silence that followed, unrepentant to see that dull mark appearing on his bronzed cheek, 'I recall *that's* something I forgot to give you yesterday.'

The smile he smiled, she didn't like. 'I really do feel, Cally Shearman,' he said smoothly, 'that the punishment far outweighs the crime.' He was right, of course, it hadn't been that much of a kiss. 'Permit me, *cara* Cally, to redress the balance.'

And while she hadn't an earthly idea what he was going to do, though it had crossed her mind before that he had looked many times as though he'd like to hit her, she didn't think he was going to return the compliment she had just served him.

Even so, she took a hurried step away, then discovered he could move faster than she could. And it wasn't to hit her that he came after her. In a flash he was up to her, and the next thing she knew, she was in his arms, and that mouth that had touched hers yesterday was over hers again.

But this kiss could in no way be compared to the previous one. Struggling like fury to get away, Cally was fighting too the spell of that mouth, that mouth with its sensuous bottom lip over hers.

She didn't want to kiss him back—she didn't. But, dear heaven, what was happening to her? She felt safe, secure, in his arms, yet she shouldn't be feeling that way.

'Don't!' she gasped, managing to pull her mouth away, but only to have it recaptured, only to have those arms tighten about her. She tried to wrench free, to pull her body away from his as he pressed her close up to him. Then she was amazed to feel a riot going off in her of more new feelings.

She was no longer struggling, but more dazed, when finally he let her go, and she found she was staring dumbly into eyes that appeared to know everything that had gone on inside her, and how mind-blowing she had found the experience.

'Did you not suspect you had such emotions inside you?' he murmured softly, the upper hand his—showing in the gleam in his eyes at her obvious bewilderment.

'I . . .' she began chokily, then was aided by a sudden fury that he was laughing at her naïvety, and was spitting at him something that had only just come to her, but which was the answer to all her problems, making her wonder why, for heaven's sake, she hadn't thought of it before. She must have been mind as well as bodily weary.

'You can keep your money—I don't need it!' She saw his eyes narrow, at her tone as much as by what she was saying. 'First thing tomorrow I shall go to the British Consulate. That's what they're there for,' she said, praying she was right, 'to help stranded Britons.'

Her fury affected him not one whit. And she just knew she was not going to like what was going on behind those clever eyes, although he seemed casual as he lodged against the table, resting his hands on the edge.

'Aside from there not being a British Consulate in Durango,' he said, studying the toes of his shoes. 'Your family still owes mine, *señorita*.'

He looked at her then, ice in his eyes at variance with the casual air he wore as he let her know that in his view that debt had to be paid before he would agree to her leaving. And then he was straightening from the table, ignoring the determination in her look that said she'd find a Consulate if it took all the small supply of money she had in coach fares to do it, and he was telling her in no uncertain fashion:

'You take one step off my property, little Miss Nose-in-the-air, and I will have your brother in jail before you can take a seat on any aircraft.'

'*Jail!*' Her determination to leave evaporated into nothing. 'You can't,' she gasped. 'You—don't know where he is.'

'I have contacts—some idea where he went. It shouldn't be too difficult for the police to pick up an Englishman.'

Far from wanting to find her brother, at the out-and-out ruthlessness on Javier's face, Cally could wish Rolfe would stay hidden for ever, as she bit down her fear, and challenged:

'You have nothing on him—he's done nothing wrong!' And that was another mistake, she thought, as she saw the chiselled look with which her words were received.

'We will leave the moral argument, since you are obviously tarred with the same brush,' he told her icily.

'Suffice it to say, I can soon think of something that will
have him kept in police custody until his case is heard.'

'But . . .' She felt swamped at the deadly earnest of
the man. 'A good lawyer would soon show him up of
being wrongly accused.'

'Maybe so,' he conceded harshly. 'But not before he
has experienced life in a Mexican jail.' And while she
was trying to come to terms with that, he enlightened
her further as he ambled to the door, opened it and
waited for her to go through. 'Our laws are somewhat
different from those in your own country. Here, a
person is guilty until proved innocent.'

And as like an automaton Cally went forward,
stunned, not believing that the hot-blooded male who
had kissed her could so soon turn into this cold man
with ice in his veins, he looked over her standing in the
doorway, and remarked offhandedly, seeing for himself
the effect his words had on her:

'Did I mention that our court calendars are crowded?
Your brother stands to languish a very long time in
jail . . .'

Cally made it back to her room without knowing
how. She was stunned, too stunned to rail and rant
against Javier Zarazua. He had her beaten—and he
knew it. And she—she had no choice but to obey his
every order if Rolfe was not to know what the inside of
a Mexican prison looked like.

CHAPTER SIX

FOR three days Cally's thoughts against Javier Zarazua were of the acid-drop variety. At mealtimes she didn't speak to him if it could be avoided, and if he looked to be getting fed up with her, then she was heartily glad. She would far rather eat in the kitchen with the others anyway.

Matters were not improved any either in that he was insisting she follow the doctor's orders to the letter, and rest. And after those three days, Cally was itching to get stuck into something.

On the fourth day since Javier had spelled out the vile consequences that would befall Rolfe if she stepped one foot off the property, Cally sat on the patio sipping her morning coffee, and got round to musing that there were some compensations for her enforced idleness. For one thing, she was getting to know the rest of the people in the house better.

Teresa had actually volunteered a smile yesterday, and that had to be a plus. For as far as she could tell, Javier was the only person able to charm a smile from the severe-faced housekeeper. Nature had been kinder to Arturo, her husband, in that she had given him a good-humoured face so that, although he was as like his wife with his sparing smiles as a matching bookend, his face was less off-putting. Rosa had to be Cally's favourite. They were getting on famously despite their lack of a mutual verbal language.

Cally had a break in her thoughts when Rosalinda, as she did every morning, came out to see her. Having remembered that the lovely child was four years old that day, she dipped into her bag and handed her

Rolfe's favourite brand of milk chocolate that she had brought with her thinking it might not be available in Mexico. It was all she had to give, but Rosalinda took it happily, clutching it in both hands as she scampered off indoors, the call of, *'Mamá!'* as she went telling Cally where she was going.

Catching a glimpse of Manuel, Cally went back to her musing. She was used to seeing Manuel about the place, and had felt a shade uncomfortable in that he seemed to be forever looking at her through his sleepy eyelids, but she had discovered there was nothing to worry about from those constant eyes in her direction, having realised it meant nothing more than that he wasn't used to seeing people with her very blonde colouring. He never stayed anywhere very long, apparently, and had picked up a smattering of English in his travels, which came in useful from time to time.

He was in the kitchen when Cally went to return her coffee tray, receiving the usual protest from Teresa for her trouble, before Rosa with her ready smile came to thank her for Rosalinda's chocolate.

'My pleasure,' Cally answered, and tried hard to comprehend the burst of Spanish that left Rosa, that had something to do with a festival.

'Rosa ask you party,' said Manuel, his large brown teeth much in evidence, as he again proved himself useful.

If she had got it right, Cally thought, delighted, she was being invited to Rosalinda's birthday party that afternoon. With help from Manuel, and more signs from Rosa, she learned that she had got it right. And after accepting with alacrity, she left the kitchen with the happy knowledge that she had at last got the promise of some sort of activity.

Rosa's hours seemed to be flexible, and since she was

not working that afternoon, it was arranged that
Manuel would take Cally to the cottage on the estate
where she and her husband lived. Promptly at three
she climbed into the rickety van, that with its lack of
paint and hoarse-throated engine appeared to her more
ready for the scrap heap than to take him around the
country.

They were slowing down, the clump of cottages in
sight, when as he changed gear, Manuel's podgy hand
brushed along Cally's knee. Knowing it was accidental,
her mind more on the help she hoped Rosa would allow
her to give, Cally gave him an easy smile and thought
no more of it, her mind back on the party and of at last
being able to do something.

'*Hay* take *casa*,' said Manuel in a mixture of Spanish
and English, as she got out of the van. And Cally was
too busy sorting out that he must mean he would come
and give her a lift back to the house to notice the way
he was almost licking his lips in anticipation.

'*Muchas gracias*, Manuel,' she accepted, and left him
to go to the cottage he had pointed out where Rosa and
Pepe lived.

But her hope that she might be able to help was
doomed from the moment she entered Rosa's charming
cottage. For there was an army of women there—a
child's birthday party in Mexico must be a very big
event. Cally realised this even before her eyes goggled at
the enormous three-tiered birthday cake. She had never
had a birthday party in her life, but had been to one
just before her mother had died, and the cake, from
what she remembered, had been nothing like this
concoction of white icing, pink icing, and yellow chicks,
figuring on every tier.

Rosa beamed a welcome at her, making her feel a
very special guest, and was soon steering her away from
the kitchen and through to the garden where tables and

chairs, some begged and borrowed from neighbours, Cally guessed, were set out in readiness, and children, brightly clothed in every hue, already having a whale of a time.

There was ample to eat, and Coke by the gallon. A tray of individually wrapped gifts was tucked away in a corner, which she learned would be presented to each child as they left.

The party was well under way when some of the family-loving men returned early from their labours. And it was then that the cry of *'Piñata!'* went up. And Cally was spellbound to see that a life-sized figure of a clown, complete with a large red nose, made from newspapers and topped wth various shades of crêpe paper, was produced.

Rosa had introduced her husband Pepe, and it was Pepe, the slim dark-eyed Mexican, not much taller than Rosa, who had the children crowding around him when he tied the solid-looking paper clown to swing from a clothes line.

Never more fascinated, Cally watched while Rosalinda was then handed what looked like the handle from a broom. Then everyone began to chant and sing, *'Dale, dale, dale, No pierdas el tino, Porque si lo pierdes, Pierdes el camino,'* as the tot Rosalinda struck blows at the paper figure. Parents grouped round as the hitting stick was passed from child to child, each child taking several whacks at the solid paper figure, one little boy letting go all the aggression in his young soul by taking vicious swipes at it before the stick was taken from him and then given to another child.

The climax of this event was reached when after first the legs of the clown and then his arms had been brutally amputated, one child gave the dummy a hefty clout, and all manner of sweets and candy fell from the head. This resulted in such a comical free-for-all, as the children dived in to pick up as many of the goodies as they could, that Cally's grin widened and she burst out laughing.

It was a joyous sound, a sound rarely transmitted from her. She felt someone at her elbow and realised, her laughter receding though a happy smile was still on her face, that someone had just arrived and that she was blocking the way.

She turned, her beautiful mouth still upturned. Then as she recognised the late arrival as Javier Zarazua and saw his eyes were fixed on her smiling mouth that had barely opened to talk, let alone smile in his company, these last few days, her smile disappeared.

'You are enjoying the *fiesta*?' he queried, appearing not to notice the effect seeing him there in this happy atmosphere had on her.

I was, she thought. Why did he have to come and spoil it? Her cool reserve, that hadn't had an airing all day, came out in full force.

'Very much,' she said coolly. But she wasn't any longer, she was now ready to leave the party, her enjoyment spoiled because he was there. 'Excuse me,' she said stiffly, politely, and made to move away from him. She would say her goodbyes, then start back for the house—she might meet Manuel on the way.

But her intention to separate herself from Javier did not come off. For she found, when she reached the proud parents of the happy Rosalinda, that he was right there beside her, and being very warmly welcomed by both Rosa and Pepe.

She waited for a break in the flow of Spanish between the three, then told Rosa as best she could how very much she had enjoyed the party, and said goodbye to them, fully expecting Javier to stay talking to them. He did utter a few words, but was soon in step with her, his hand firmly on her elbow as they walked through the speculative-eyed parents, Javier exchanging a greeting here and there as they went.

What the devil did he think he was doing, grabbing hold of her arm like that, and in front of all those people making it look as though he was her escort? She fumed—and lost no time once they were inside the house in shaking off his hand, ready to give him a chilly goodbye.

'I'll probably see you at dinner,' she said, with a fine air of dismissal, and saw from his stern look that he wasn't liking her very much.

'I'm taking you home.'

'No, you're not. Manuel is coming for me. I'm going to w . . .'

'Manuel is not coming for you. And you are not walking anywhere in this heat,' he countermanded, with arrogance that annihilated hers.

'I've arranged with Manuel to . . .'

'And I've told him to get on with his work.'

Oh, God, how she hated him! Cally thought angrily as, forced, or face being frogmarched, she went out to his car. Moodily she wouldn't look at him as he got in beside her. But he did not start the car straight away, which had her having to look at his grim face when he made no move to set the car forward.

'In future, you will go nowhere with Manuel—Is that understood?'

She had no intention, other than accepting the corpulent Manuel's kind offer of a lift, of going anywhere with him. But that didn't stop her answer from being immediate, and fiery, at what she saw that all Javier Zarazua was interested in was spoiling her smallest pleasure.

'Who do you think you are?'

'I'm the man who'll be supplying your air fare,' he told her shortly, another indication that she had to jump to his tune.

'And don't you just love to rub it in!' she snapped,
and saw his hand bang down hard on the steering wheel
just as though she provoked him beyond endurance.

'Stay away from him!' he thundered, and was
viciously stabbing the car into motion.

The return journey was completed in less than half
the time Manuel had taken, a heavy silence like a
fortress between them.

Her surmise that she would see Javier at dinner, was
erroneous, Cally discovered. Though, seeing a light
under the study door, having learned he spent many
an hour in there, she thought he must be having a
working dinner while he caught up with his paper
work.

And a good job too, she thought. Better he should
stay locked in his study, it saved her the necessity of
putting up with him more than she had to. Oddly,
though, she had little appetite for her meal, and it
couldn't be put down to what she had eaten at the
party, for she had eaten very little.

Her mood of rebellion stirred itself the next morning.
She was sick and tired of Javier Zarazua laying down the
law with every breath. Another long day of inactivity
yawned in front of her.

Feeling fidgety, it was about eleven that morning
when, kicking against Javier's decree that she should
rest, she began to think that even cleaning the overseer's
house would be better than doing nothing. She was on
the patio when she saw Manuel come round the side of
the house. She should, she thought, apologise to him if
he had got into hot water from Javier yesterday, and
she crossed the lawn about to do just that.

Having made her apology, she saw from Manuel's
brown-toothed smile that he held no animosity. 'Drive?'
he said, which she thought meant he was going into
town for something and was offering her a lift. He had

a piece of wood in his hands, so perhaps he needed some screws or something for it.

Regretfully, she shook her head. She wouldn't forget in a hurry what Javier would be instrumental in doing to Rolfe if she set foot off his property. But rebellion boiling up in her, and Manuel's offer of a lift into town gave her another idea.

'You take me,' she said, pointing first to herself and then him, 'to overseer's *casa*?'

'*Si—si*,' said Manuel at once, giving Cally cause to think how nice of him that he wasn't holding it against her that Javier had given him the rough end of his tongue yesterday.

'*A momento*,' she said, having no idea if that was right.

It conveyed to him all she wanted to say anyway, she thought, as with a happy feeling of blow Mr God Almighty Javier Zarazua, she breezed into his study where she had seen a rack holding keys.

It didn't take her long to recognise the label she had seen before on the key to the overseer's house. And with an attitude of mentally thumbing her nose to him, Cally went to race out to where Manuel usually parked his van. But it was a thoughtfulness in her nature that had her going by way of the kitchen instead of across the patio and cutting across the lawns and round to the side of the house.

Teresa looked up when she went in. 'Overseer's *casa*,' said Cally gaily. 'Manuel's taking me there.' And when Teresa looked at her blankly, she went over and showed her the label attached to the key in her hand. Teresa's response then was agitated and vocal.

'*No! No!*' she exclaimed, raising her hands aloft, regardless that one held a dripping wooden spoon.

'*Si—si*,' giggled Cally, heading for the door. Let her tell Javier, why the heck should she care!

She would get those curtains hung up today, she thought, as she sat down beside Manuel and he took off, ignoring the fact that Teresa had come out and was giving him a mouthful of Spanish.

Once more during the drive Manuel's podgy hand brushed her knee. But the easy smile that lifted her mouth as she turned to him faded abruptly as she saw that his eyes looked positively leering.

I'm mistaken, she thought, some of her elation dimming. She moved nearer the door, even though she was sure she had imagined that look in his eyes.

But the slight feeling of unease had her jumping out of the van, wanting to avoid any conversation with him the moment he pulled up at the overseer's house.

'*Gracias*, Manuel,' she called, not wanting to hang about.

She had picked up the correct key, she discovered as the padlock undid, and she went inside. The downstairs was just as she left it, but feeling full of energy, she stopped by the kitchen for the curtain fastenings, and with her sights set on getting those curtains up at the windows, she went upstairs.

She was in the process of dividing the fastenings for each curtain, when a sound had her turning. 'Fun, eh, *señorita*?' said Manuel, before her brain could catch up and tell her just what he was doing there with his fat podgy hands going to the buckle of his trouser belt.

Alarm ripped through her, as feeling sick, she averted her eyes, her throat dry. Oh God, she could scream her head off and nobody would hear her.

'No, Manuel,' she said, trying to make her voice sound firm. 'You have it all wrong.'

'*Si,*' he said, and didn't appear to have heard at all, as he laughed, those lascivious eyes mentally stripping her as with elephantine movements he lumbered nearer.

Spurned to action, her eyes wide as he undid his belt,

Cally was over the bed and to the other side, her eyes going to the window even as memory came that that particular window had stuck when she had tried to open it the other day.

'No. No fun,' she said, while she calculated that she was far nippier on her feet than he was—if only she could keep some space between them. If he made a grab for her, caught her, then her strength just wouldn't be up to a victorious fight against his solid bulk.

'*Si,*' he was saying, '*fiesta.*'

So he wanted a party. Her eyes never leaving him, Cally caught hold of a curtain rod. It wasn't much of a weapon, but it was all she had.

She saw him look at the puny object in her hand, and heard his coarse laughter. Then suddenly, as his laughter died, she thought in the still silence she heard a faint purr of a car engine. Hope rose, but she was too terrified that if she went to the window to look out and found there was no car near, Manuel might make that grab for her. He hadn't heard anything, she could see, as he gradually came nearer and she saw the lustful look in his eyes.

And then he stopped. He too heard the roared shout of, '*Cally!*' followed by the pounding of footsteps coming up the stone stairs.

Her heart was bursting with relief, tears spurting to her eyes as Javier lunged into the room, a look of demoniacal fury on his face as he swept one enraged look to her defending herself with a flimsy curtain rod, and on to the suddenly blabbering Manuel.

What Manuel was trying to get across Cally had no idea—that she had led him on, probably, she thought. But Javier wasn't interested in explanations, it seemed. For with a roar like that of a wild bull, he pulled Manuel from the room and from her sight, and from the thumping, banging and yelling that came back she could only guess what went on.

There was no thought in her mind, despite Manuel's weight, that he would get the better of Javier. All she knew then, warmth for her employer coming to her, was that he had appeared from nowhere to save her.

Seldom had Cally allowed herself the luxury of tears, but her release from fear manifested itself in great choking sobs she just did not have any way of holding back.

Tears were pouring down her face when in a very few minutes Javier came back. She heard the hoarse engine of Manuel's van start up, so she knew Javier hadn't killed him, as had looked likely. And she knew she just wasn't in control of herself as tears still falling, she ignored the grim look of him, and helplessly cried:

'Javier—oh, Javier! It was all my fault. I—I didn't understand—I should have known . . .'

Through her tears she saw the grim look fade. Then in a very few strides Javier had her in his strong comforting arms, a soothing hand smoothing up and down her back as he led her to sit with him on the bed.

'What experience have you had to know these things?' he murmured softly, his one hand still soothing while the other cradled her head to his shoulder.

'I sh-should have known what he was like,' she sobbed. And not needing an answer, because the intelligence was there, 'You suspected . . . That's why you told me to go nowhere with him, wasn't it?'

Quietly he hushed her, and tried to calm her. 'I have sent him on his way, it is all over now. Do not think of it.'

'I'm—sorry,' she wept, and was hushed again.

But emotions that had for years been kept rigorously under control were out of their usual conformity and were not so easy to gather again into any sort of alignment. Reserve was a thing of the past as, needing

every ounce of comfort the security of his arm about
her afforded, Cally snuggled into him, her arms going
round his waist as helplessly she clung to him.

When she felt his hand leave her hair, come beneath
her chin and raise it so he could look into her eyes, it
never dawned on her that for a person who claimed she
hated him so much it was very peculiar that she should
find his arms such comfort. All that penetrated, as
she drew one shuddering breath under the searching
gaze of those blue eyes, was what a sight she must
appear to him.

'I must look a mess,' was all she was capable of
saying, as gentle fingers brushed tears from her damp
face.

'You look beautiful,' he said softly. And from
somewhere Cally summoned up a semblance of a smile
because he had once said she was beautiful when she
smiled.

But Javier didn't smile at her brave effort. His eyes
went to her smiling lips, then back to her eyes. And it
was then that he kissed her.

There was a stillness in the room. Cally was no longer
sobbing. She no longer felt like sobbing. She just
gripped on to him because something was happening to
her and she wasn't at all sure what it was. All she knew
with absolute certainty was that she definitely did not
hate this tall, fair Mexican. Which must mean that she
had to like him, because to have him gently kiss her just
didn't seem wrong.

'I think,' said Javier, breaking his kiss, a pulse
beating in his temple, his one arm as tightly about her,
as hers were around him, 'that we should go now.'

'Yes,' Cally said, but made no move to take her arms
from him, just as he was making no move to let go of
her.

'I——' he said, then looked into the large limpid

pools of her eyes. And it was then that a stifled groan left him, then that he brought his other arm into play. And it was with both arms around her that he kissed her again.

His second kiss was deeper than his first. His third kiss had her in a mind-spinning no man's land, as she kept her arms round him and met his mouth with a fire starting to kindle in her.

The feel of his hands at the back of her, caressing now where once they had been soothing, did nothing to help her out of her mindless state. Some unthought-of magic was having her hands going caressingly over his back, up to his broad shoulders and into his hair as his mouth left hers to kiss her throat, to kiss behind her ears.

She strained to him, clutched on to him when his hands came to her waist and she realised they were on her naked skin—she hadn't so much as felt him separate the material from her jeans. His hands came to the front of her, and she swallowed.

'Do not be afraid,' he whispered, his eyes on hers, his expression tender as his hands moved upwards.

Cally wanted to tell him she wasn't afraid, but was so unsure what she was, she didn't say anything. And at the moment his upward moving hands touched her breasts, his lips claimed hers, and she clutched at him again, breathing his name on a choky breath:

'Javier!'

'I offend you?' he queried softly, stilling his caressing movements, though not taking that tender hold from her breasts.

'Oh no,' she whispered back, and was pink with shyness at her own words, which she thought should have made her feel a brazen hussy, but strangely, didn't.

A smile broke in him as he witnessed the pink in her face, and he saved her any further embarrassment in

having to look at him while being so forward, by
kissing her again, while his hands moved to caress once
more, taking time out to unbutton her shirt, to undo
her bra and have her forgetting everything but the
feelings he aroused when his hands came to her once
more, to the full globes of her uncovered breasts.

Hardly knowing what she was doing, Cally felt the
same need to feel his skin. And she in turn was
unbuttoning his shirt, unthinking at his convulsive
movement as her hands took the same freedom with
him that he was taking with her.

They were still sitting, all this new to her as her hands
went from his back to his chest. He wasn't hurrying her,
but the urgency growing in her for him had her wanting
more, yet more. She felt his lips on the hardened peak
of her breasts, and wanted to feel his skin against hers.
Then she discovered he had read her need, for
regardless of the curtains on the bed she had laboured
over, Javier was pulling her close to him, her breasts
against his hair-roughened chest and his arms round
her, his body coming over hers as in a gliding
movement he was moving her to lie down.

To feel his hardness against her, that same raging need
in him she felt, had her heart hammering, as hoarsely he
murmured, *'Te quiero,'* as he pressed himself to her.

'What—does that mean?' she choked, only then
beginning to feel any sort of nervousness.

Tenderly Javier smiled down at her, 'I want you,' he
translated. And on a breath, *'Te amo.'*

Cally didn't get to hear a translation of *'Te amo'*, for
she saw suddenly the fire of wanting in his eyes, and
nerves she had thought she could quieten wouldn't be
quieted, as they disclosed themselves, just when he was
going to kiss her again, in the most frustrating nervous
cough.

Desperately afraid she was going to go off into one of

her coughing sessions, she pushed at the chest against her, and found on an instant that Javier was helping her to sit up.

The coughing attack didn't happen. But as his hands came to fasten her bra, to cover her with her shirt—she had no idea when he had taken it from her—and to button it up, she knew she had ruined everything.

'I'm . . .' She had been going to say she was sorry, but it wouldn't come as she saw the way Javier was buttoning up his own shirt. And it was then that the reserve she had always known crowded in.

But as she made herself look at him, into those eyes that only seconds ago had been aflame with desire, she saw nothing there to indicate that he found her the most infuriating woman of all time. His expression was rueful, she saw, as he referred openly to that tickle of a cough that had had them breaking apart.

'You do pick your moment, Cally Shearman, to remind a man that you have recently been ill and need rest!'

'I . . .'

How could she now tell him she was feeling fine? A few minutes ago she had felt she could tell him anything, but that had been before that reserve of her upbringing had plunged in and taken her. The girl she now was, inhibitions safely intact, would not dream of giving him such an open invitation.

'H-how did you get to—to be here?' she questioned, needing to take her mind away from what so nearly had happened, from what she had wanted to happen.

If Javier had observed she had resumed her touch-me-not mantle, for once he didn't take exception to it. And if he was remembering that not too long ago she had lain pliant in his arms, but now looked to be wanting to dissociate herself from that warm, giving person, then that too he made no mention of, choosing then to take her up on her 'let's get on to a nothing subject, and fast' question. Though there was a secret smile about him, which gave her to think he was getting to have an understanding of her that she would rather he did not have.

'I returned home to make a phone call about a business dinner I have in town tonight,' he explained easily. 'But before I could get anywhere near my study, Teresa was running to me with the news that you had just driven here with Manuel Ireta.'

As Manuel's name left him, so she saw his expression harden, saw in him again traces of the man she thought she had hated. But for all that hardness in him, he managed to keep his voice even as he said:

'You can see what happens when you disobey me, Cally?'

Cally wished she could be as hard as him, wished she could find that earlier mutiny in her soul to tell him she wasn't some submissive female, even if his order that she stay clear of Manuel Ireta had proved to be justified. But she had received a very real fright, and there wasn't a scrap of mutiny about her.

'I've said I'm sorry,' she said stiffly, hoping he would leave it there. He did, to her surprise, but had a question of his own to ask.

'Why did you come to this house at all? I would have thought my home far more comfortable.'

'I—like it here.'

'You are saying you do not like my home?'

'It—isn't that,' she said, struggling, wanting rebellion, mutiny, to help her out.

'What, then?'

'I wanted—something to do. I feel well again now, full of energy.' And as the realisation came to her, she was blurting out in wonder, 'I haven't coughed for days now,' but went scarlet as she recalled that tickle in her throat at that most inappropriate of moments.

It was too much to hope that Javier hadn't witnessed the rosy glow in her cheeks. But if he had been frustrated himself on being forced to remember his opinion that she had been ill, then there was none of his frustration showing. Unbelievably, as she witnessed that he too had remembered that small untimely cough, she saw it had had the effect only of restoring his good humour. And he was actually grinning when he said:

'We shall have to do something about that—nervous cough,' leaving her to gather all sorts of things from the implication behind his remark.

Hastily she went back to the subject they had been discussing. 'I'm—I'm not used to being idle,' she said quickly. 'I wanted something to do.'

Fortunately, it looked as though she had succeeded in getting his thoughts into different channels. For his grin had gone, and though that hardness didn't return, there was a sternness about him as he said:

'You will not come here again.'

Cally did not answer. If he was waiting for her to give him her word that she wouldn't, then she didn't see how she could give him her promise. Inactivity was sending her round the bend. And with the work there was here—Manuel Ireta sent on his way—she just couldn't see that she might not yet find some other way of coming to the overseer's house to get on with it, if Javier wouldn't bring her.

'You heard me, Cally?'

'I can't—promise.'

She raised stubborn eyes to his, saw he didn't care for stubbornness in a woman, but she was in the grip of it, and it would not let her go.

'Very well,' he said at last. 'Come if you wish.' Cally guessed the conversation was over, and stood up. Then she discovered he hadn't finished. 'Though I think maybe I ought to warn you, that though I have ordered Ireta off my property, the area it covers is too large for me to know should he creep back one dark night.' He paused. 'I did tell you this house has been squatted in before, didn't I?'

Cally stayed her intention to go from the room and down the stairs. Was he bluffing or was he serious? Did he really think Manuel Ireta might come back, or had he just said that to ensure she came nowhere near the place? She thought the latter, was positive of it. But even so, she knew then that she wouldn't be risking it. It was there in her face, the promise Javier wanted that she would keep away from the overseer's house.

'Lying pig,' she said, mutiny arriving late.

And she heard him laugh, as unoffended as she had been when his hands had held her breasts. 'Now is that nice, *señorita*,' he said, his grin wide, 'after *all* I've done for you!'

Cally ate her solitary dinner and went back to her room, irritated with herself that her only dinner companion had been a nagging in her to wonder if the business dinner Javier was attending was in fact business, or was he perhaps having dinner with some female who was never troubled with a nervous cough at precisely the wrong moment.

Not that she was bothered whom he dined with, she told herself stoutly. But she went to bed thinking about him, about his mocking '*all* I have done for you', and couldn't find sleep.

To her all he had done for her meant more than saving her from being stranded in Querétaro. This morning he had taken her state of girl-womanhood, and brought it on by leaps and bounds.

At midnight she heard him come in, and went to sleep. But at one o'clock she was awake again, and feeling so far from sleep, that she snicked on the table lamp and sat up.

Thoughts of Javier began entering her head again, this time the memory of the way she had cocked her head in the air and sailed past him when they had arrived back at the house. Then thoughts of him went skidding from her mind as through the open window came a fat, green, fast-flying three-inch-long insect which promptly settled itself on the headboard beside her.

With a strangled yelp she was off the bed and over by the door. The insect had moved fast, but not knowing if it had a fatal sting, Cally moved faster.

For only a second did she hesitate, and then she was through the door and along the landing and hammering on the bedroom Rosa had one day pointed out as being Javier's.

'Javier, Javier!' she shouted, trying to hold down her panic, although she had closed the door on that pale green object.

And when in seconds the door was flung open, Javier still pulling a robe over his nakedness, she was blabbering in fine contrast to the way she had been the last time she had seen him when she had opted to walk off like some imperious dowager duchess:

'Th-there's a-a th-thing in my room!'

'Thing?' He must have been sound asleep, she guessed, but at her obvious distress, he quickly came wide awake. 'What thing . . .' he started to say. Then he was putting her to one side, 'Stay here,' he instructed, and was striding off up the corridor.

But Cally couldn't allow that. She had to warn him. And she sprinted off after him. 'It's a green insect thing,' she panted. 'I don't know if it's poisonous or not.'

Without hesitation Javier opened her bedroom door.

With her heart hammering with fear, Cally went with him, and saw as he did that the insect had not moved from its resting place.

'What is it?' she whispered, afraid to take her eyes from it in case it moved. 'Is it dangerous?'

It seemed to her then an age before he answered. And it wasn't until he took his eyes from the bedhead to look at her, slender in her cotton nightdress, her haughtiness a thing of the past, her eyes transfixed by the insect, that he did answer her.

'Occasionally such monsters do find a home in peach trees,' he said quietly.

'There's a peach tree outside my window,' she whispered back, telling him what he already knew, but too mesmerised by that bedhead to be aware of such things.

'We shall have to get rid of it, Cally,' Javier said, his voice deadly serious.

'I know,' she said on a whisper.

'And you will have to be very brave,' he told her. 'Are you brave, Cally?'

She knew she wasn't brave at all. Had she been of the stuff heroes were made of, she would have walked out on her father when Rolfe had asked her to.

'Yes,' she lied. 'What do you want me to do?'

'Give me your hand.'

At once Cally put her hand into his, aware she was trembling and hoping she was the only one to know of it. Then Javier was taking her with him and up to the bedhead, and Cally broke out into a cold sweat as he lifted his free hand and stretched it forward. With bated breath she watched, wanting to run, as that hand neared the object, and braved herself to follow to the letter whatever instruction he issued.

Then, just when her nerves were one jangled mass, Javier's hand dropped swiftly on top of the insect and he gathered it in his hand. Then turning to her, his face split from ear to ear, he said:

'Poor harmless innocent planter, you scared Cally half to death!' And while she stood open-mouthed, he let go her hand and took the insect to the window, where he set it free.

Harmless planter! Cally's petrified fear broke in the most furious rage she had ever experienced. 'You swine!' she yelled. 'You lying devilish swine! I was terrified!' Her fury was too much to be contained by mere words, and like a wild thing she went for him her fists flailing.

'Oh, Cally!' She heard the laughter in him as he caught hold of her wrists. 'You lied too. I couldn't resist it. Not after you had told me how brave you were.'

'That's no excuse!' she shrieked, kicking at him with her bare feet, wriggling like fury to get free, until with an admiring look, laughter still about him, he took her calling him a 'Mexican heathen,' and replied with:

'I suspected there was passion in you this morning, little hellcat, but . . .'

'Leave this morning out of it!' she raged, ignoring that her incensed twisting and turning had upended a chair that went toppling, taking with it, with a terrific din, a solid Aztec ornament it clouted from the dressing table.

Frustration was added to fury that her attempts to make him let go of her were useless, and she kicked out at him again. Only this time, it was to discover for her pains that if she had gone out of control, then Javier had known all along how to control her.

Effortlessly, he caught the back of her knee with his bare foot, and before they could go crashing to the floor he had swung her round so that they both ended up on the bed.

Winded to find the mattress firm beneath her, Javier over her, his hastily done up robe open, Cally felt the heat of the length of his naked front penetrating the thinness of her cotton shift. And it was then that her fury died as other more treacherous emotions made themselves felt.

'Javier,' she said, and was helpless to know what else to say.

'It's all right,' he said, looking into her eyes. 'I want you the same way I wanted you this morning, but soon I shall leave. Just let me lie quietly with you for a moment to apologise for what I have done.'

What he had done was receding further and further from her mind. All she knew was that she didn't want him to go. She wanted him to stay, as she knew, as she felt his body movements, that he wanted to stay.

'I must not kiss you,' came from him as though wrenched. And it took all her power of will not to move her body beneath his, afraid as she was of causing an explosion in this inflammatory situation, since he had already stated his intention to leave her soon. 'Will you forgive me for frightening you so?' he asked, harnessing his desire when for a moment it had looked to be going out of control.

'Why—did you?'

'So many times you have looked at me with that disdainful air. When I brought you home today was not the first time. I'm afraid I just couldn't resist prolonging the moment when the warmer Cally came through.'

His answer surprised her into making that movement beneath him, and as she felt the instant response of his body, she heard him say tautly:

'Keep still, Cally, for God's sake.'

'I think,' she managed, not knowing when she had become such an accomplished liar, 'I think I want you to go.'

The smile in his eyes told her he knew she was lying. But he allowed her the lie, maybe to make up for the fright she had received. 'I think you're right,' he said, and made to move from her.

But before he could do more than lift himself to bring his robe around him, they both heard a sound by the door. Later Cally realised that if the sound of her banging on Javier's door, her yelling at him at the top of her voice not too long since had not disturbed them, then the sound of the chair going over, the Aztec ornament falling, would have been enough to waken the whole household, and some investigation was needed. But she was horrified and not thinking at all, when her eyes shot to the door to see that not only had Teresa come to investigate, but that Arturo too was standing there. They were both in their night attire and were standing as though jammed, dumbstruck in the doorway. And there was no doubting from the expression on the housekeeper's face that she at least had put her own interpretation on what the Señor was doing in her bedroom.

Then before Cally could utter a sound, and Javier, although he had seen both of them, was making no effort to explain about the insect, without saying a word, as one, Teresa and Arturo left the doorway and disappeared from sight.

That was when Cally's shocked vocal chords found release, but they had gone. And it was with some heat that she rounded on Javier, as with his robe now round him, he allowed her to sit up.

'Why didn't you say something?'

He shrugged. 'What was there to say?'

'They think—they think we've—were—have lain together,' she spluttered.

'And we haven't?' The mocking lift of his left eyebrow was the last straw.

'Not in the way they think we have,' she said hotly—
and wasn't sure she would not have physically gone for
him then if he said one word of what was written on his
face—that it had been a near thing that morning.

'It worries you what Teresa and her good husband
think?'

Cally recalled Teresa's unsmiling face, recalled the
one or two smiles Teresa had sent her way, and knew
which she would prefer.

'Yes,' she said. 'Yes, it does.' And she knew then,
from the way Javier's face took on a thoughtful look,
that he was going to say something that would either
have her hitting him, or have the effect of shutting her
up.

'All right,' he said with an indifferent shrug, 'if the
opinion my housekeeper and her mate have of you
worries you that much—I'll marry you.'

CHAPTER SEVEN

WHEN Cally awoke to another glorious day, she was to wonder at what had gone on the night before. Then recalling the, 'That worried, I'm not', with which she had rejected Javier's carelessly offered 'I'll marry you' before, entirely unaffected at being turned down, he had paused only to right the chair and return the ornament to the dressing table, before sauntering casually from her room, she ceased wondering, and left her bed knowing that some time she was going to have to come face to face with the housekeeper.

As expected, dark looks were the order of the day. Even Rosa, who was always bright and cheerful, seemed affected by Teresa's unsmiling, snappy countenance, the vivacity of her smile seldom peeping out that day.

When Rosa went home, Cally went up to her room to use some of the ample time at her disposal in washing her hair, and in wishing there was some magical way in which she could be transported to England. Teresa's face had been as black as thunder all day, and even Arturo had succeeded in looking down in the mouth.

Was this how it was going to be until she had earned enough to pay her air fare? And how was she going to earn any of it, when Javier was insisting she be treated like a semi-invalid and not allowing her to do anything?

Her hair was shining with health and vitality when she put on her one long dress, now becoming as many times washed as the rest of her wardrobe, and was then ready to join Javier for dinner. Always supposing he didn't have a business dinner tonight, she thought disconsolately, the way Teresa had been with her today having got through to her. And always supposing he hadn't got pressing paper work that had him taking his meals in his study.

But Javier was not dining out, nor was he in his study. Cally saw him about to start mounting the stairs, just as she reached the top of them. Aware that he was watching her every step as he stood there at the bottom of the staircase, his eyes on her shining blonde hair, not to mention the sudden flurry of pink that stained her cheeks on the memory of his body burning over hers in her thin nightdress, Cally had nothing to say until she was on a level with him.

'I was about to come and collect you,' he offered, a smile there in his eyes as he looked at the receding blush that had covered her.

'Oh!' she exclaimed airily, while wondering why she couldn't be like other girls and treat what had happened between them lightly, without that thumping in her heart region starting up from the moment of seeing him. And, mustering all her cool, 'You're dining at home tonight, then?'

The smile went from his eyes in an instant at her haughty attitude, and it was in no uncertain terms that he grated, 'Stop it, Cally!'

She knew what he meant, but pretended she didn't as she tried to hang on to her pose. 'Stop it?' she queried, and would have floated past him then, her head in the air, if he had been in a mind to let her.

His hand snaked out settling in a firm grip there was no getting away from, before she had taken more than one step. Disdainfully she looked down at that hand on her arm, then up to a pair of scorching blue eyes.

But he had the anger she had aroused in him under a

tight control, she saw, even if it was through his teeth
that he bit:

'That blush that just covered you tells me the natural
Cally Shearman is the warm, full-blooded female I have
a few times held in my arms.' It caused her to feel
flattened that he could refer to something she would
never have chosen to discuss. 'So come down off your
arrogant perch, Cally Shearman,' he instructed. Then
all at once his smile was there again, and with his left
eyebrow arching upwards, he added after a pause,
'Unless, of course, you'd like me to do something to
flush that full-blooded woman out of hiding?'

Her assumed arrogance tumbled, went crashing to
the floor. 'I'm—er—naturally reserved,' she excused
herself, knowing he wasn't joking—he'd soon flushed out
the woman in her before, it mustn't happen again. 'And—
and,' she collected herself, 'don't think I'm being arrogant,
but—twice in—er—your arms was more than enough.'

'You can't count,' he corrected.

But he was no longer smiling, though he seemed to
accept her reserve was as natural as her blush had been.
And his hand fell from her arm as with that same hand
he indicated the door of the dining room.

'Dinner does seem a better idea,' he said coolly.

And with Javier being cool, and with Cally more fed
up than ever, and hiding behind her cloak of reserve, so
the mood was set for a not very friendly dinner.

Matters weren't helped that when Teresa came in to
serve, she had a smile to spare for neither of them. So
that having toyed with meat and vegetables she didn't
want, Javier was unequivocally scowling at Cally when
the housekeeper departed.

'What the devil's the matter with you?' he rapped, the
moment Teresa had closed the door.

'Nothing,' she muttered, and saw her answer had him
near to exploding.

'Like hell it's not! You've eaten barely enough to keep a sparrow alive—have avoided looking at Teresa every time she has come in.' Silently he fumed for a second, and was then thundering, 'Are you such a wishy-washy creature that you cannot accept that even you have feelings that can make you forget your frigid upbringing on occasion? Is that what's wrong with you?'

Cally threw him a look of seething dislike. 'I'm not wishy-washy,' she hurled back, the colour of anger staining her cheeks.

She might have thought so once, but she had learned differently since leaving England. But he had fired an anger in her she hadn't known, until she had gone for him last night, that she possessed. And with him looking at her furiously, clearly not believing she hadn't been tearing herself to pieces at the reaction he had stirred in her, she went on to blaze:

'And if my appetite is poor, then what else can you expect, with Teresa looking as though she hopes anything I eat will choke m . . .'

She broke off, horrified at what she had said. For though he sat tight-lipped, the look of fury suddenly went from Javier, and she had a terrible suspicion that all she might have succeeded in doing by losing her temper was to get Teresa into trouble.

'Teresa?' he queried. 'What has she to do with this?'

Wriggling uncomfortably, Cally stared down at the lace tablecloth. 'It's—it's not Teresa's fault,' she said, seeing that it looked like being the housekeeper's turn for some of his wrath if she couldn't smooth things over. 'We both know she's a devout and Christian woman with a very high moral code.' And going on hurriedly, 'She must have been scandalised by—by what she saw—thought she saw last—night.'

'Ah,' he said softly, 'I see.'

And when she looked at him again, she was seeing something too. Javier Zarazua had that alert look in his eyes that told her his brain was working overtime.

'Teresa has been giving you the cold shoulder treatment she is noted for?'

'It doesn't matter,' Cally said quickly, suddenly realising there had been no need for her to get hot and bothered about Teresa getting into trouble. After all, they were both his servants, even if, so far, she had only been allowed to do a couple of days' work.

She was just about to change the subject, to tackle him about her lack of employment, remind him that the sooner she started work, the sooner she could remove herself from his household, when Javier himself changed the subject.

'Tell me, Cally,' he opened conversationally, 'some more about your life in England.'

So he accepted that it didn't matter if Teresa glowered at her from dawn to dusk, she thought, feeling a twinge of disappointment, although it had never been her desire that he should take the devout woman to task.

'I think I've told you all there is to tell,' she replied, not attempting to bore him by retelling the little there was to tell.

'You have told me you kept house for your father,' he agreed. 'But surely there is more than that.'

'It was a very . . .' she sought for a word, trying to avoid the word "dull", and saw him smile when she brought out, 'wishy-washy' life.'

'No boy-friends?'

She wished she could say yes, but remembering the spotty youth who used to live next door who had wetly kissed her in the garden one day when her father was out, and had trembled at the knees when she'd stared wide-eyed, not having liked the experience at all, she discovered that experience came in handy in that she was able to say:

'You weren't the first man to kiss me.'

And Javier was back pretty smartly with, 'But you haven't put in much—practice?'

He had kissed her and, expert himself, must know she had a lot to learn. 'I'm—er—not up to championship class yet,' she replied flippantly, and was lost to know where this conversation was going when he asked:

'But you don't have one particular—coach—back in England?' Blankly she looked at him, and saw he wasn't looking particularly interested in her reply anyway, as he asked, 'You are not in love with anyone in your own country?'

The door opened, and a disapproving Teresa was back with them. 'No,' Cally answered his question. But she saw that though her answer had registered with him, he wasn't as she suspected at all interested, for the smile on his face was for Teresa only as he said something to her in quick Spanish, which Cally could not understand a word of.

Then she saw Teresa turn and look at her and realised then that he must after all have taken her to task for being surly. Because suddenly Teresa was beaming the widest smile she had so far directed at her. And not only that, she was coming round the table to her, words pouring from her in excited Spanish as she took her hand and shook it vigorously.

And it was not until she had gone, saying something that sounded as though she had to tell Arturo something, that a few of the words she had rattled in her ear disassociated themselves from the rest of her excited chatter.

'What ...' Cally was fairly reeling in her astonishment. 'Teresa said something about the—the Señor's *novia*!' she gasped. And, not believing that what her brain was deciphering could in any shape or fashion be true, 'You didn't—you *didn't*—tell her that I—I was your fiancée, did you?'

The way Javier Zarazua managed to look back at her without looking in the least abashed did nothing in the way of helping Cally get over her mind-boggling amazement.

'I thought it would please you,' he replied pleasantly.

'But—you—I told you last night I wouldn't marry you,' she said, still incredulous, not sure now what she had said in reply to his offer, but sure she had left him in no doubt . . .

'Last night was different,' he said coolly, going on, 'I admit I was hasty to suggest last night that we marry—I had not thought then what I would do had you agreed.' So he would have been kicking himself this morning for his impetuosity, Cally thought, her mind still reeling. 'But I have said nothing today about marrying you.'

'But—you did tell Teresa that—we are engaged?'

'*Si*,' he said briefly. And before she could tell him he could jolly well tell Teresa that they weren't engaged, he was going on, his tone hardening, 'But you know as well as I that engagements are easily broken.'

It stopped her in her tracks to know he was remembering her brother's treatment of Graciela. And she had confirmation, if she needed it, that he had not for an instant forgotten the dishonour served to his family by one of the Shearmans, that being the cause for the hardness in him being resurrected, when he said stiffly:

'I would appreciate an amicable agreement between us as to when our engagement should be broken, rather than hear, like Graciela, that my betrothed has absconded—much rather than that everyone should know that I too have been jilted.'

She still wanted to tell him she had no intention of

being party to a phoney engagement in the first place, but what he had said had the effect of bringing her up short.

It was *already* too late to deny it if she didn't want to bring shame on his family a second time. Teresa had rushed from the room to tell Arturo within minutes of hearing the news. And with no restriction being placed on Teresa using the phone, she had looked excited enough to even now be ringing up half of Durango.

'Damn you, Javier Zarazua!' she threw at him.

'What have I done?' he asked innocently.

'You know damn well what you've done!' she snapped. 'You know I can't deny the engagement, not without . . .' She stopped, realising with those words she had committed herself to go through with it. And she knew he had realised it too, when the hardness left him, and his lips curved. And there was a world of charm in him when, leaning back in his chair, he drawled softly:

'I only did it for your protection, sweet Cally.'

The next morning Cally waited, as was her habit since she had been what Javier termed 'ill', to hear him go out before she thought of presenting herself downstairs. She was in no hurry to see him again, even though she knew she must to get some idea of exactly when their temporary engagement would be terminated.

She knew it was useless to tear herself to shreds fretting and fuming about this new position she found herself in—she had done enough of that during the sleepless night hours, and the situation was just the same this morning. She must have been so stunned at finding herself actually engaged to him, she thought, that she had not thought then and there to question how long the farcical engagement should go on. Either that, or so swamped by the feeling that whatever happened, his family should not receive a second humiliation from the Shearman family.

That meant, of course, she meditated, blinking at the way her thoughts were going, that she was on the way to believing what Javier had said of Rolfe was true. She frowned, unable to credit that the Rolfe she knew, wild at times admittedly, should propose to a girl and then jilt her on learning that she was not the prospective heiress he had believed. Though jilt Graciela he must have—the wedding hadn't taken place, had it!

On going downstairs, Cally found that the greeting she had received yesterday bore no comparison with today's greeting. Gone were the glum expressions that had met her the day before, as a beaming Teresa, and an overjoyed Rosa, all too obviously having been informed of the Señor's engagement, broke into excited talk at her appearance. Rosa came over to wring her hand, the look on her happy smiling face translating the accelerated Spanish that accompanied her blissful look. All too plainly, Rosa thought her betrothal to the Señor highly romantic.

Gradually through the day, the *casa* settled down to normality. But if Teresa was trying to make up for the rare appearance of her smile in the past, then Cally couldn't go anywhere near her without that severe face being relieved by a parting of a smiling mouth.

As a result, the happy atmosphere in the house was getting through to her, and by the time lunch came and went, she was beginning to feel less upset. And it was midway through the afternoon, Teresa resting while Rosalinda napped and Rosa did some ironing, that crossing the hall, carrying some ironing to her room that Rosa had refused to let her do herself, she came face to face with Javier.

Reserve rose, and about to remark that she had not expected to see him until dinner time, Cally opened her mouth, then found she was being soundly kissed, which did nothing at all to quiet the sudden energetic pumping of her heart.

Unable to push him away with the ironing in her arms, she backed a step, about to go for him, but was prevented by seeing the very devil in his eyes as he murmured:

'We have to keep up appearances, Cally.'

'Er—of course,' she mumbled.

But on turning to look behind, she could not see a sign of Rosa, if that kiss was meant to indicate that Rosa had been watching.

'You . . .' she began, about to get it straight here and now that she wasn't going to get into the habit of allowing herself to be kissed without any good reason. But she was halted by his laughter, by his comment of:

'Stop looking so serious, *niña*, it wasn't much of a kiss.'

'Is that how you see me—as a child?' she couldn't help the question, that sprang to her lips.

Javier smiled, that wicked look still there in his eyes as he rocked back on his heels. 'Reserved, inexperienced you may be, little Cally,' he said, seeming to be in high spirits, 'but even you must be aware that I have regarded you as a fully grown woman when I've held you in my arms—that fully grown woman confirmed in your response.'

If he had been looking for a way to prevent her from arguing, if he had been aiming to seek out her blush, then Cally did not disappoint him on either count. A pretty pink suffused her face, and not one question did she have to ask him then.

'I'll—see you at dinner,' she choked—then discovered the reason why Javier was not out on the range with the men as she had supposed.

'I came home specially to see you,' he said, before she could move towards the stairs.

'To see me?' Now why should her heart hurry up its
beat at his words? Defeated to know the answer, she
concentrated, until it dawned on her that he must want
to talk about those same questions that burned in her.
'Oh, of course,' she said, 'we never did get round to
agreeing when our—when to announce that we weren't
going to get married, did we?'

Before her eyes, his good humour deserted him.
'We'll talk in the *sala*,' he said abruptly, disregarding
her bewilderment at the change in him. It wasn't, she
thought, because he had taken exception to what she
had said, because even if Teresa or Rosa were in
earshot, which they weren't, they would not have
understood her language anyway.

'I'll just take my laundry to my . . .' she tried.

Then she saw she had upset him with a vengeance, as
he took the freshly ironed clothes from her arms, and
with a no-nonsense look about him, not relieved when a
pair of dainty briefs slithered from the top and he had
to bend to pick them up, he very nearly threw her
neatly ironed laundry down on the stairs.

'We'll talk now,' he muttered, and had taken her by
the arm and was propelling her to the large *sala*, where,
it seemed, he was doing his best to get over the sudden
ill humour she had somehow sparked off.

'This has been my first opportunity to give you this,'
he said evenly. And while she stood watching, her eyes
going huge, he dipped into his pocket and drew from it
a ring case, which he then opened and extracted the
most magnificent diamond solitaire ring she had ever
seen.

Speechlessly she stared at the bright winking object in
his fingers. 'It—isn't n-necessary for . . .' she stammered,
only to be cut off by his terse:

'It is very necessary. The first thing Teresa is going
to look for tonight is the diamond ring a Mexican

always gives to his future *esposa*.'

Future wife! But she wasn't going to be his wife!
Cally's thinking at that stage was all shot to pieces, her
thoughts that this had gone far enough, that she
wouldn't wear his ring, never being heard as with a
gentleness totally opposite to his mood, Javier took
hold of her left hand and pushed the ring home on her
engagement finger. And before she knew it, she was
softly exclaiming:

'Oh, Javier, it's a beautiful ring!'

Her remark seemed to have pleased him. Or perhaps
it was just satisfaction that he had subdued her
opposition to wearing it, she thought, for she had made
no move to take it off.

'A fitting ornament for a beautiful hand,' he said
gallantly, keeping hold of that hand he had just
described as beautiful.

But Cally was coming to her senses, and pulled her
hand free, too aware of his warm skin next to hers. And
Javier, making no move to hold on to her, let his hand
drop to his side and was ready for her opposition, small
though it was when it came.

'Will Teresa really expect to see me wearing a
diamond at dinner?' she asked.

He nodded. 'Not only that, she will expect me to go
flying off to England to ask your father's permission.'

'You can't do that!' The words rattled from her in
hasty exclamation, to be received with an arrogance
that was all proud Mexican as he rapped stiffly back:

'He would object, your father?'

Cally dropped her eyes. She doubted her father
would be that much interested. Though no father could
want more for a son-in-law than the tall, well-to-do
Mexican anyway. And she saw the truth then, just from
the way Javier had taken charge of her, had seen to it
that she didn't do a thing, seen that she rested after that

bout of exhaustion, that when the time came for Javier to take a wife, that wife would be well looked after, cherished. No, no father could object to handing his daughter over to his safe keeping. She raised her eyes, saw the pride in him as he waited for her answer.

'No father would object to you,' she said quietly. 'Certainly not mine.' And realising she was getting altogether too soft, 'Is that the custom in this country, then—for the—er—prospective bridegroom to seek the father's permission?'

Again he nodded, and she was relieved to see that the proud stiffness had left him. 'Though it is not the prospective groom who asks for permission, although he of course is present. It is the custom here for the father or brother of the happy man to go to speak for him.'

To Cally, it seemed a delightful if maybe formal custom, and asked a question that she realised, if she had thought about it, it would have been wiser not to ask, since every time Rolfe's name came up it always ended with Javier being short with her.

'Did Rolfe go through this custom for . . .' Her voice tailed off. Already she was wishing, as his mouth tightened, that she hadn't got started.

'He did,' he stated coldly. 'In the absence of your father or a brother, he impressed my cousin's priest with his sincerity, and got him to act for him.' And while she was taking that in, he succeeded in firing her instinctive defence of Rolfe, by snarling, 'We both know how sincere your brother's feelings for Graciela were when she told him she could not expect money of her own.'

'My brother . . .' was as far as she got.

'Is a louse,' Javier finished for her icily. And before she could go for him again, 'I will see you at dinner.' And she was left standing there. All too clearly he was not interested in a word she would have said in defence of Rolfe.

Though what she could have said to defend him, since she only had the facts Javier had given her, Cally didn't know, as up in her room she sat on her bed and stared helplessly at the flawless diamond on her hand. Tears crept to her eyes and escaped down her cheeks. Oh, what a mess! Here she was temporarily engaged to a man who loathed the very sound of her brother's name. And she had nothing to defend Rolfe with, but the certainty in her that Rolfe, wild though he sometimes was, even idiotic on occasion, had never ever been money-minded. It just wasn't in her to accept that he was like their penny-pinching father. She just refused to believe that.

'Ah, *bonita*,' beamed Teresa, forgetting for a moment that she was supposed to be serving Cally with soup, as she stood by her chair in the dining room that evening, and admired the ring adorning her finger.

Cally offered her a smile, for in truth there wasn't much else she could do. But the smile soon disappeared the moment Teresa had gone. She was aware that Javier who had been held up on a phone call and had joined her not many minutes ago, was looking at her, but she had no mind to look at him.

'Something has upset you?' he quietly, firmly enquired.

'Where would you like me to start?' she asked acidly, flicking a disgruntled glance at him.

'You've been crying,' he observed quickly, ignoring her acid, his voice softer now as he probed, 'Why, Cally?'

She didn't want to answer, though she knew she was going to have to. They were only on their first course. Somehow or other before the meal was over Javier would find out why she had shed tears; she had learned that much about him.

'I'm not sure I know myself,' she sighed helplessly. 'You, me, Rolfe.'

'Your brother?' It was there again, that short sharp tone.

'Yes,' she flared, 'my brother.' And exasperated suddenly, 'Every time his name comes up you get all— nasty!'

'With justification, I think,' he said contentiously. Then, his brow thoughtful, he went on more evenly, 'This makes you cry? That I am—nasty—about your brother?'

'I'm not responsible for his crimes,' she snapped, scoffing at the very idea that he had any power to upset her.

'You are admitting, then, that he is guilty of what my family consider a crime?'

'No. No, I'm not.' Some of the heat was going from her that he was maintaining his even tone—that, Rolfe still under discussion, he hadn't returned to being short with her. 'Whatever else Rolfe is, he isn't interested in money—he just isn't. I know him.'

Just as she knew Javier would never believe a thing she said in Rolfe's defence. Convinced of that, she was astonished when after a moment of thinking over what she had said, he brought out:

'I have had to re-think my opinion of you, Cally, I may have to take more time to change my opinion of your brother.' And as he smiled at her astonishment that he was prepared to reconsider what he thought of Rolfe, he added, that wealth of charm he had evident, 'Will it make you happier if I agree not to get "nasty" the next time your brother is spoken of between us?'

His charm was a potent force, causing her to wonder that she didn't seem up to making any reply save for the briefest inclination of her head. And she had a few minutes to continue wondering that his charm had got through to her, when just then a smiling Teresa came in to serve the main course.

'You—er—mentioned you had re-thought your opinion of me,' she found herself fishing the moment Teresa had gone.

'My opinion that you were here for what pickings you could get?' he queried. 'My apology for that is long overdue, I fear.' And with that charm again, 'Are you going to forgive me, sweet Cally, for harbouring such vile thoughts about you?'

'You no longer think ...' He was shaking his head before she could finish.

'No, I don't,' he said, but he gave no clue what he did think.

And the next time he spoke, it was on a different matter, so what he thought of her could not have been so very important, she realised. Though what he said next had her forgetting the odd despondency that had started to settle.

'We must decide soon on which date we are to have our engagement party,' he said out of the blue.

'Engagement party! But—there's no need for that, surely?'

For a second there, it looked as though he was going to go tight-lipped on her again. He then looked at her with those sharp eyes that had earlier picked up signs that she had been weeping. And his voice was level when he replied:

'I'm afraid there is. Many times today I have been congratulated on my good fortune. That phone call before dinner was someone else with good wishes—the news that we are engaged is everywhere.'

Her heart sank at that. But still she had to protest. 'But it's ridiculous to have a party when we both know that the engagement is to be broken—that I won't be here long.'

'You are thinking of going somewhere?' His hold on the evenness of his temper was slipping, she could hear it in the sarcasm that came through with his words.

'You know I am,' she snapped, rattled. 'As soon as I've earned—And that's another thing. How am I ever to earn my fare to England, when all I do is loll about doing nothing?'

'You have needed to rest. You . . .'

'Well, I don't need to rest any more,' she flared, her own temper shot. And, fed up suddenly, she was pouring out the lot. 'Here I am stranded in a country not my own, fit and eager to do something to earn my fare home, yet every offer I make to work is denied. I came here to work, but apart from those first two days I haven't done a stroke,' she complained, and still having some steam left, tacked on, 'And as though that isn't enough, my return ticket never looking like appearing, I suddenly wake up one morning and find I'm involved with you in some farcical engagement without the remotest possibility of getting out of it, because—because . . .'

'Because?' he questioned, insisting that she shouldn't stop now.

'Damn you!' she blazed. 'How the hell can I deny it? Your family have suffered enough humiliation from my family.'

'And that bothers you?'

'Wouldn't it bother anyone with an ounce of decent feeling?'

'You are admitting your brother is lacking in decency?'

As promised, he wasn't getting nasty that Rolfe was again in the conversation, which surprised her even if it was Javier who had brought his name into it. But she was wary. There was that sharpness in him that told her she would very soon see that tight-lipped angry expression, and as suddenly as it had blown up, her anger subsided.

'Can we leave my brother out of this?' she asked wearily. 'We only end up fighting when his name comes into it.'

She saw the alertness in his eyes, and wanted then only to go to her room. 'You don't want to fight with me?' Javier asked, intrigued.

Feeling dejected, Cally shook her head. 'No, I don't.' She didn't. She didn't want to be submissive either, but, unused to verbal fighting, she had discovered rowing with him upset her. 'All I want to do is—is get out of here, and go home.'

He was a long time in replying, so that she thought he was not going to answer, that he wasn't after all interested in any of what she had said. But it was as she was pushing an unwanted piece of chicken around her plate that he ended his silence, a pleasantness in his voice she hadn't been expecting.

'It is impossible for me to immediately announce that our engagement is at an end—with everyone now knowing of it I think you will see that.'

'Yes,' said Cally quietly, wanting herself to avoid the talk that would be on the boil for days if they said they had changed their minds within twenty-four hours, not counting having to suffer Teresa returning to the scowling woman she had been yesterday.

'But,' said Javier, 'I think we will be able to do away with the party. I can let it be known that you are not yet fit enough for such excitement.'

Feeling as strong as a horse, since she had started this whole thing by being against a party in the first place, Cally just didn't have one leg of objection to stand on.

'Thank you,' she mumbled.

'And since you are so eager to return to the land of your birth,' he went on, his voice still retaining that pleasantness, although when she flicked a glance at him she could see a certain hardness in his eyes, 'I propose, subject to your agreement, of course,' was he being sarcastic? She didn't know, but she stayed quiet and heard him out, 'that we stay engaged for—three months. We can then announce that we have made a mistake, and I will then purchase your air ticket to England.'

'Three months!' was the only thing she had against any of what he had said.

'You agree?'

'I—agree,' was dragged from her. Though as she thought of those long idle months ahead, she just had to ask, 'And I can go back to work?'

'It is not fitting for the fiancée of Zarazua to perform domestic duties,' he told her, a wealth of pride she knew she wasn't going to get past there in his voice. And then he smiled, and she was on the receiving end of his charm again. 'But, if you wish, you can help me with some of my paper work.'

Cally took to Javier's office work like a duck to water, discovering that her lack of expertise in his language was no obstacle, in that a good deal of his business was with companies in the United States. It was this side of the business in which he instructed her.

Her typing, albeit the two fingers variety, was coming on too, she thought two weeks later, feeling far happier than she had ever expected to be.

And if, because of that happiness, her reserve was melting, then that was something to be pleased about too. No longer did she hesitate to enter Teresa's domain, the kitchen, but felt as welcome there as anywhere. Teresa had a special warmth for her these days, and Cally was hopeful it was not just because she was engaged to the Señor.

She was now allowed to sample Mexican food too, though nothing that was over-spiced, and lunch most days now consisted of *tortilla* done up in various ways; with beans called *frijoles* and cheese, and called *tacos*; *tortilla* fried and topped with meat, mild chili, tomatoes and lettuce, and called *tostades*; a folded *tortilla* stuffed with meat, cheese and sauce and called *enchiladas*. But her favourite so far, as was the cinnamon-flavoured coffee, was the large non-hot variety of chili that was filled with cheese before being dipped in beaten egg and cooked.

Cally glanced at herself in the bedroom mirror before going down to begin work that Saturday. Javier had said there was no need for her to work today, but she knew he had handwritten some letters for her to type back on Monday. Might as well do them today, she thought, and smiled back at her reflection, noticing that she was collecting a bit of a tan and that it suited her. Then she was musing on the patience Javier had shown when instructing her on paper work procedure.

She came away from the mirror, her thoughts with him. He had not kissed her since that day she had had her arms full of laundry and had been unable to prevent him. But she recalled that day he had come home early when she had been in her ancient swimsuit from schooldays, sunning herself by the pool.

'I *have* been working,' she said, having finished all he had left for her. And she had smiled as she said it, because it had sounded as though she felt guilty to be caught taking a breather.

'I'm sure you have,' he had answered with a grin, his eyes going over her long shapely legs, the rest of her in her navy swimsuit that should have been thrown out long ago. 'But we're all allowed a few perks.'

The way he had said it, the way he had stooped down, his face close to hers, had given her a very real impression that he was hinting he thought the fact they were supposed to be engaged entitled *him* to a few perks. She had thought then, as his head had come nearer, that he was going to kiss her.

But it was the knowledge that came to her, that she wouldn't mind a bit if he did, that had her getting quickly up from the lounger, with a husky, 'I think I'll—go and—and have a shower,' as she headed indoors.

Javier's laugh had followed her. She had thought it a pleasant sound, and could only wonder then what it was about the man that made her insides act up the way they did.

Cally left her room, taking with her the tray Teresa still insisted on bringing up to her room early each morning, regardless that she had tried to convey that she would rather she didn't.

'*Buenos dias*, Teresa,' she called gaily, and saw Teresa's smile for her as she replied to her greeting. She then made her way to the study, her gaiety dipping as she thought of the hours it would be before she saw Javier that evening.

She opened the study door, and had no time then to wonder why she should be upset that she might not see Javier before she joined him at the dinner table. For he was not out with the stock as she had been sure he would be, but was there in the study, his expression so deadly serious as he placed the phone in his hand back on the receiver that she had to know that something very dreadful had happened.

'What—is it?' she asked quietly, making no attempt to go over to her usual seat at the desk, her face as solemn as his.

For what seemed an age, Javier said nothing, but just fixed her with a stern look from those bright blue eyes. And suddenly, the longer he took to tell her, Cally just

knew that whatever had gone wrong, it somehow had
something to do with her.

'What's gone wrong?' she asked, all her tensions
knotting together. 'Something has happened, hasn't it?'

Sternly he nodded. 'Your brother,' he said at last,
'has been injured.'

CHAPTER EIGHT

ALARM clawed at her. For the moment stunned, all Cally was capable of was staring at Javier, emotions in her declaring that whatever Rolfe had done, or was said to have done, he was her brother, and she loved him. Then as Javier led her to sit down, one question bubbled to the surface.

'Is—is he seriously injured?'

'He will survive, I have just been told.'

Through her agitation came the thought that he didn't sound too pleased that Rolfe would make it. But this wasn't the time to have a go at him about it. He had said Rolfe would survive, and that was all that mattered.

'I want to see him,' she said, a stubborn look about her.

'Naturally. I will take you to him.'

'You know where he is?' Of course he did, had probably known for some time, she guessed, but she didn't pursue that either. 'Is he in Durango?'

'He's in hospital in Mexico City. You'd better go and pack a case. We might be there a few days.'

It hadn't passed her by, even though her first thoughts had to be for Rolfe, that Javier was sounding exceedingly fed up. She realised what he had said then, that he would take her to Rolfe, and something softened in her. Javier worked hard, the ranch took up a lot of his time, yet here he was offering to leave his beloved home, leave his work for a few days—she couldn't let him. Between them the Shearmans had intruded much too much.

138

'There's no need for you to take me. I can go on my own,' she said, leaving her chair and making for the door.

'I have said I will take you,' he said sharply, the matter as far as he was concerned settled. All he was waiting for was for her to go and get packed so they could get on their way.

But at the door Cally paused, a thought hitting her, disappointing her that he had so little trust in her. Did he think that, like Rolfe, she would walk out on her engagement?

'I'll—come back,' she promised, wanting him to know his distrust was unfounded.

'That's true—with me,' Javier told her grittily, just as though he thought, despite her promise, she might go and not return, leaving him with another load of dishonour to face. 'I have business to conduct in Mexico City. Next week is as good a time as any.'

With Javier being in a non-communicative mood, the stiffness of reserve Cally had hoped to have said goodbye to for ever was back with her. So that it wasn't until they had landed in Mexico City, Javier offering a tight-lipped, 'You'll want to go to the hospital straight away,' that safe in the knowledge Rolfe would 'survive', she was able to unbend to discover how her brother came to be injured.

'Yes, please,' she said stiffly, as Javier escorted her from the airport to a waiting hired car. And when their luggage was in the boot and he came round to take the driving wheel, 'Can you tell me how the accident happened?'

'Accident? Who said it was an accident?' he questioned, his eyes on the mêlée of cars that appeared to block every exit as he spun the wheel and found an opening.

'It——' Cally felt herself growing pale. 'You mean it—wasn't an accident? That his injuries were inflicted—deliberately!' Good God, no!

'Serves him right for running off with a married woman,' was the unsympathetic response, causing Cally's world to spin round her ears at the thought—was there no end to what Rolfe was supposed to have done?

Swallowing hard, she just had to know more. 'You're saying his girl-friend—the one he—he left Graciela for—is married?' And as what he said sank in, 'You're saying—the woman's husband beat him up?'

'If I know Yolanda Nolasco's husband, he'd get someone else to do his dirty work—several, I shouldn't wonder.'

'But that's unfair!' she exclaimed heatedly, sickness invading her at the thought of Rolfe's handsome face being . . . He didn't answer, though she had a shrewd idea he thought Rolfe deserved everything he got—more, probably.

When they reached the hospital, Javier left her in the reception area while he went to make enquiries. Cally knew she owed him, and then some, but she could not help the fact she wasn't liking him very much at that moment. There were several people sitting about on chairs, convenient cigarette butt troughs liberally scattered about, no restrictions on smoking apparently, causing her to wish that if the habit could do anything to salve frayed nerve ends, she had a few packets herself.

'I will take you to his room,' said Javier, striding back to her, his hand coming to her arm.

The ward Rolfe was in was high up in the massive building, but having escorted her that far, Javier made no move to go in with her.

'I will wait for you,' he said, a chilly look on his face

that told her, this far and no farther would he go.
Though thinking from the look of him, his first sight of
the man who had jilted Graciela might have Javier
finishing what had been started on Rolfe—make his
chances that of the non-survivor type—she thought
perhaps it was a good thing he had no stomach to see
her brother.

There were about six beds in the ward into which she
walked. Some of the patients sitting up and taking
notice, only one of them flat on his back. She
approached the bed, Rolfe's thatch of blond hair the
only distinguishing feature on the swollen face, split lip
and mass of bruises.

'Oh, Rolfe!' she cried. 'What have they done to you!'

'Cally! Cally—good grief, where the hell did you
spring from?' Speech was painful to him, but his
astonishment on seeing her there, when he thought her
still in England, had him ignoring his pain in those
initial moments.

More interested in hearing about him, she gave him a
very potted version of how she had arrived for his
wedding, heard from him that he had not received her
letter, and told him she had kindly been offered a job
by Javier Zarazua until she had earned enough to pay
her fare home.

'You're working for Javier Zarazua!' he exclaimed,
wincing as his split lip looked like cracking further open.

'Do you know him?'

'I've heard of him,' said Rolfe. 'Wouldn't have
thought he'd have given any of my kin a helping hand,
though.'

'He's been very kind,' Cally told him. 'And that's
enough about me. More importantly, how are you
feeling?'

'How do I look?'

'I've seen you look better,' she said cheerfully,

wanting to cry at the mess that had been made of his face.

Because talking was so painful to him, she didn't stay long that first visit. Gently she kissed him goodbye, but she didn't know how she kept the tears from falling as she left the ward.

She was blinded by tears as she closed the door after her, her mind full of Rolfe's poor battered face and the cracked ribs he had told her about. She had no idea where she was going as she set off down the corridor. And it was through a haze of tears that she saw Javier standing in front of her.

Without saying a word, he just stood, his eyes on her face that battled for control. Then Cally felt the security of his arm at the back of her as he turned her and kept his arm about her as he walked her to the lift. That arm was still about her, not one word having been said, as out of the lift they came and he placed her to sit in the passenger seat of the hired car.

'We'll book into a hotel first, then see about having something to eat,' he stated, getting into the car beside her.

Not hungry, Cally felt too choked to answer him. And she had still not said a word when he parked the car in the hotel's underground car park and took her with him to the desk to arrange their accommodation. Then once more they were travelling in a lift.

He had booked them into a suite of rooms. And, not having moved very far from her side, once the porter had been dealt with, he went to inspect the bedroom accommodation, coming back to deposit her suitcase in the room he had selected for her. Then he was back, and had his hands on her arms, and was looking down into her eyes.

'I had a word with the doctor while you were visiting,' he said, his face grave. And as her grey-green eyes stared solemnly into his, one side of his mouth began a slow curve upwards. 'He's going to be fine, Cally, just fine.' Still she stared solemnly at him. 'The doctor told me he should be out of there in a couple of weeks—now they wouldn't be talking of letting him go so soon if there was anything seriously wrong with him, would they?'

The tight grip she thought she had on herself began to waver. She sighed, deeply, just once. 'Oh, Javier,' she said, then crumpled and began to cry. 'He—he looks so t-terrible!'

Hauled into his arms, she howled her eyes out, crying out all her shock on seeing Rolfe so badly treated. But at last, still in the security of Javier's arms, her tears dried and she began to grow a little ashamed that she had had a good go at soaking his shirt.

'I never cry, so why is it always you I blubber all over?' she sniffed, taking hold of the handkerchief he was dabbing at her eyes with, and doing her own mopping up.

'Perhaps it's because I'm always in the right place at the right time,' he teased.

And it was in that moment that she made a tremendous discovery, was shaken to her foundations to discover that the way her emotions played havoc with her, that sexual awareness of Javier she had put it down to, was much, much more than that. In that moment of those teasing blue eyes looking down at her, Cally knew herself in love with him.

Shock rocked her that this was the reason for her hammering heart on too many occasions—occasions when she was not in his arms, not being kissed by him, when all he had to do was walk in the room and her heart would start thumping. Cally just stared at him.

'Are you all right?' His teasing grin had gone. 'You've lost some of your colour.'

'I'm fine,' she lied, backing out of his arms. 'It's—just the shock—the shock of seeing Rolfe like that. I . . .' She made a supreme effort and got herself together. 'Do you mind if I not bother having anything to eat? I'm not at all hungry.'

She hadn't thought he would agree—he'd watched her appetite like a hawk in those early days. 'Why not lie down for an hour?' he suggested. 'I have some appointments to make which could take me all of that time.'

Needing to be by herself, she thought it was the best suggestion she had heard in a long time.

It was more than a few days they spent in Mexico City. And if Cally had hoped her love for Javier would prove to be just a figment of her imagination, then in the days that followed, days in which she fell deeper and deeper in love with him, she knew that had been a vain hope. In a little over two months she was going to have to part from him—and she had no idea how she was going to be able to do that.

Their days had fallen into a pattern of Javier going off early to meet his business associates, but he always came back to take her to the hospital to visit Rolfe. He never offered to come in with Cally to see her brother, and respecting how he felt—hadn't he done more than enough, to fly with her to Mexico City within an hour of receiving the news? she never asked him to. After her visits to Rolfe, he would then drive her out of the city, always to somewhere that would have taken her mind from her brother and what had befallen him.

On Sunday, Javier had driven her to the spa town of Cuernavaca, said to be Mexico's oldest resort. From there they had driven on to the silver-mining town of Taxco, the prettiest of hill towns. On Monday it had been to Guanajuato, a city with the most fascinating underground road network, that spread right under the city. It was there that Javier had pointed out the house where Diego Rivera, one of Mexico's most famous painters, had lived.

From Guanajuato, he had taken her to San Miguel Allende, a place known for its artists' colony. It was in San Miguel that they stayed and had dinner. That was when Javier had said, 'Now what can we do to tempt your appetite?' Her lack of appetite had not gone unnoticed by him, but because she wanted to please him, she had tried hard to fancy eating something.

'I think . . .' she began, trying her own hand at teasing, since she knew that what she was about to request was impossible, 'I could eat a pizza.'

She saw from his face that he had noted the sparkle in her eyes. And for one moment, in that night-time crowded square, the town's whole population, it seemed, taking the air, Cally thought, as his head came nearer and her heart began to pound, that right there he was going to kiss her.

The smile on her face faded, her eyes going serious. She wanted him to kiss her, but she was afraid—afraid she might cling to him for a moment too long, that he would guess her secret.

But although his face was close, Javier did not kiss her. Instead he let his forefinger trail lightly down her cheek, then was teasing back:

'Then pizza it shall be, my lady.'

And while she still thought he was joking, he steered her from the bustling Square and down a hilly street, halting only when they came to a building with a sign that stated, *'Mama Mia'*.

'Inside or outside?' he asked, with a grin at her dumbfounded expression.

'Er—outside,' she opted, feeling quite heady just being with him.

Together they shared a giant pizza brought to them on a platter. Together they sat at a bare wood table in the open courtyard. And because a pizza was what she had requested, there in the candleglow, the table's only decoration, Cally ate every scrap of her share. And then and there as she sat with him under the whispering leaves of a overhanging tree, apricot she thought, she knew she wasn't certain of anything any more save that she couldn't fall any deeper in love with Javier—her love for him consumed her.

By Tuesday there was a marked improvement in Rolfe. The swelling in his face had gone down, and he was now able to walk about the ward a little. And since it was less painful now for him to talk, Cally thought it about time she heard some of the story from his own lips.

Though not knowing where to begin, she was glad that Rolfe himself showed no lack of inclination in bringing up Yolanda's name, when in answer to her remark that another week in hospital would see the bruises on his face disappearing, he said, with brotherly candour:

'Stuff that! I'm not staying here a day longer than I have to.'

'But the doctor said . . .'

'Don't fret, Cally,' Rolfe butted in, with the best he could do in the way of a smile. 'I won't do anything stupid.' All semblance of a smile went from him, as he told her, 'But with Yolanda waiting for me in Acapulco, I want to get there as soon as I can.'

That he was in no condition to travel anywhere, much less Acapulco, which must be miles away, Cally thought, as headstrong as he was, he must surely see. Though knowing him of old she knew there was nothing more guaranteed to have him trying it than any comment anyone made to the contrary. So leaving that aside for the moment, she decided to concentrate on Yolanda.

'It's serious, then—this thing with Yolanda?' she asked tentatively.

'You bet your life it's serious,' he replied. 'God, do you think I would have broken with Graciela at that late stage if it wasn't?'

Many thoughts fought for precedence then, but since he seemed prepared to openly discuss it, Cally told him the first thing that came into her head, though she was careful not to alienate Rolfe to Javier in any way, by avoiding bringing him into it.

'Graciela—her family, the Delgadillos, thought you'd —thrown her over because she told you her father was only manager of the engineering works—that they haven't any money to speak of.'

'Good God!' Rolfe exclaimed, looking stunned. Then, quickly recovering, 'They're a proud lot—I expect they thought that up rather than have the true story put round.' He gave her a sharp look. 'You didn't believe it, did you?'

'I couldn't,' she said simply, her eyes shining that her trust in Rolfe was vindicated. Then a shadow came to cloud them. 'Though the poor girl was dreadfully upset that you left it so late to tell her you'd changed your mind.'

'Far better for her to be upset now than for us to marry and for me to go off with Yolanda at a later date.'

'Yolanda was the cause of your breaking your engagement?'

Rolfe nodded. 'I met her soon after my marriage was arranged. I thought I loved Graciela, I truly did,' he said earnestly. 'But within minutes of talking to Yolanda, I knew she was the only woman for me—even though I tried not to break faith with Graciela. I tried,

Cally, I honestly tried. But I kept bumping into
Yolanda accidentally—it was the only time I came
alive. She was unhappily married to a pig of a man—I
saw the way he was treating her, belittling her. in
company. And I just couldn't take it.'

'So you ran away with her.'

'Nothing would have stopped me once I knew she felt
the same way about me. But I knew there would be
difficulties.'

'Her husband came after you?'

'And how!' muttered Rolfe, rubbing his chin
reflectively.

'Between us Yolanda and I had enough money to
last us a year. But after hiding for a few weeks, I thought
we'd better come to Mexico City where I might stand a
chance of getting a job. Yolanda was sure her husband
would follow us, and sure enough, one day in the Zona
Rosa, she spotted one of his brothers.'

'Oh, why didn't you run . . .'

'Run away?' He gave her that twisted smile. 'I love
Yolanda, want to marry her. I couldn't, Cally, spend
the rest of my life running.'

'But Yolanda went to Acapulco.'

'And don't think it was easy to persuade her to go,'
he smiled again. 'She can be a stubborn little cuss,' he
said fondly. 'But if there were to be any fists flying, I
didn't want her to be in the way—Yolanda discovered I
can be as stubborn as she can.'

'Does—does she know what has happened to you?'

'That the Nolasco brothers descended *en masse*? Only
the barest details. I phone her every day.'

'And she's expecting you to join her in Acapulco.'

'I don't want her in Mexico City until I'm certain the
Nolascos aren't around. And that's enough about
them,' he said, and went on to talk of Yolanda, of how
Cally would love her too, if the two ever met.

Cally could see that her brother absolutely adored Yolanda, and because she was heart and soul in love herself, she could only hope that one Shearman at least found happiness in the love that had come to them uninvited.

Before her visit was over she told him, even though he had not asked after their father, of his intention to marry Elma Bates. 'They're probably married by now,' she ended.

'Well, I hope he makes her happier than he made our mother,' Rolfe declared. Which gave Cally something to think about as she left the hospital.

Rolfe was five years older than she; he would remember, where she couldn't, the life her mother had had with her father. If it had been anything like the joyless existence her own life had been, she mused, then there had been little happiness in their marriage.

'Something wrong—Rolfe?'

Javier stepped round from the car, parked in a different place from where he usually parked it. It was the only time he had ever used Rolfe's first name, and the unhappy thoughts in Cally cleared like magic. Just seeing Javier, just hearing him speak her brother's name without animosity had stars in her eyes.

'He's fine,' she said, then amended, 'Well, he's getting better.'

'You—seemed upset.'

'Oh, I was just thinking of something Rolfe said.' He made no move to go and open the car door for her as had become his habit, but was waiting for her to continue, waiting for her to tell him what had made her look upset, was dragging the words from her, 'He—was telling me about the—grim time my mother had with my father before she died.'

'Your life wasn't a bed of roses either, was it?'

She hadn't told him that, had she? 'Roses are such

thorny things, aren't they, most uncomfortable-sounding,' she said lightly. And when Javier gave her a penetrating look, her bright manner clearly not deceiving him, Cally added, 'Your opinion that Rolfe didn't marry Graciela because he found out about the firm belonging to you was wrong, by the way.' She saw the icy coldness come to his eyes, but went on nevertheless, 'He fell so much in love with Yolanda, he just couldn't do anything else but . . .' She was talking to herself. Javier had gone and opened up the passenger door.

With Javier looking so grim as he drove out of the hospital gates Cally wouldn't have been at all surprised if he had taken her straight back to their hotel and dumped her there. So it was a welcome surprise, since she wanted to spend every possible moment with him, to see him get in among the tangle of furious traffic, then take a road that led out of Mexico City.

'Where are we going?' she asked hesitantly, wanting him back to being the easygoing companion he had been these last few days.

When he didn't answer she thought it was because he was feeling too ill-tempered to want to talk to her. Weak tears filled her eyes, as she turned her head, her chin tilted proudly, to stare out of the side window. Then, as suddenly as they had come, those tears dried. For it seemed Javier had made a supreme effort to get over his bad humour.

'Fancy seeing some ancient pyramids?' he questioned, his voice if not exactly friendly, then thankfully, not hostile.

'Could we?' she exclaimed, turning to him, her shining eyes smiling. 'Where? Are there some near here?'

'Teotihuacan,' he said, flicking a glance at her, his good humour restored on seeing her eager, happy face.

Teotihuacan Cally found breathtaking. The splendid site had two huge pyramids, the smaller, though still mammoth, being the pyramid of the moon, the larger and better preserved being the pyramid of the sun. There were other historical buildings to see too, such as the temple of Quetzalcoatl, all to be found by walking along a wide avenue named the Street of the Dead.

But before he would let her walk anywhere, Javier insisted on stopping at one of the many nearby stalls that sold everything from Mexican wall rugs to onyx chess sets, and purchased for her a straw hat which, with due ceremony, he placed on her head, then stood back to admire the finished effect.

'Cute,' he pronounced, and Cally laughed, and determined then not to think of what was to happen in two months' time.

She found him a wonderful guide, able to answer her every question—'Did the Aztecs live there? Who was Quetzalcoatl?' And many more—so she just knew, since archaeology wasn't his subject, that he must have visited the site before.

And yet he made no attempt to hurry her, climbing with her the steep steps up the pyramid of the sun, seeming prepared to stand in the hot sun for as long as she wished to admire the view of open countryside, until Cally remembered that while she had a hat on, Javier was bareheaded.

Going down the sloping steps of the pyramid looked to be a tricky exercise. And since she had no head for heights it saw her wondering which foot to put first, until Javier noticed her dilemma.

'Hang on to me,' he instructed, and was offering a rock-firm arm as a banister.

'Thanks,' said Cally when to her relief they had reached the bottom.

'You wanted to climb up,' he teased.

'Wouldn't have missed it,' she laughed, and thought she would burst with happiness that he was back to teasing her again.

Going to bed at night proved no problem, although since they shared the same bathroom, Javier, who usually stayed up late either reading or seated at the small desk in the room, couldn't avoid seeing her flit by in her dressing gown.

'Goodnight, Cally,' he would say in an easy sort of way, and wanting desperately to linger, she would offer him the best she could in an easy goodnight of her own.

On Wednesday Rolfe seemed to have made yet another stride in his recovery. But to her relief, he made no mention, as he had yesterday, that the hospital weren't going to be able to hold him once he felt fit. Perhaps he's not feeling as good as he's trying to make out he's feeling, Cally thought, and left the hospital with the idea in her mind to try and find the courage to ask Javier to have a word with the doctor for her.

That afternoon he took her to the floating gardens at Xochimilco. And all thought of asking him anything to do with Rolfe went from her mind as the romantic setting took over.

Together they sat in a paper flower-decorated wide punt, and were poled along the waterway, passing floating flower sellers, people on craft selling steaming food. But Cally's delight knew no bounds when a band of *mariarchi*, musicians hatted in the wide sombrero of Mexico, came along side and Javier, after one look at her entranced face, settled their fee, and they began to play.

'That was wonderful,' she breathed as, their boat trip over, Javier helped her ashore.

'I thought you might like it,' he said, but with such a casual air it set her wondering if he had liked it too—or was finding the whole experience boring beyond belief.

'Y-you don't have to—to take me around, you know,' she said flatly. And at his sudden look as though to say, 'What's come over you?' she went on hastily, 'I mean, if you're bored to tears . . .'

'Did I say I was bored to tears?'

'Well, no—but . . .'

'If you don't behave yourself,' he said, back to teasing again, she was sure, from the light in his eyes, 'I won't take you to the Folklore Ballet to-night.'

'Tonight?' she exclaimed, having heard of the fabulous Folklore Ballet, but unable to believe she was actually going to get to see it!

'Their performances are usually held on Wednesdays and Sundays,' he told her.

'Oh,' she said, and added uncertainly, 'By Sunday you want to be back in Durango?'

'My business will be finished by then,' he replied, making no mention of Rolfe.

'Yes, yes, of course it will,' said Cally. But she was quiet on the way back. If it was a choice between staying on here and going back with Javier to Durango, with Rolfe looking so much better, then her heart was telling her which she would rather do.

A thunderstorm greeted them in Mexico City. And because she liked to watch thunderstorms, when Javier parked the car, even though there were stairs leading from the parking area into the hotel, Cally couldn't resist going outside to have a look.

Vivid forked lightning split the sky, and knowing no fear, she was startled when a rough hand grabbed hold of her arm, and Javier rapped:

'Haven't you any more sense?' then hauled her after him into the hotel.

He was still angry with her when they reached their suite, his furious eyes looking down to where rain, the like of which she had never seen before, had plastered her dress to her. Not a foot away, she saw his eyes on her breasts, the material of her dress moulded to her.

Then, as though someone else was in control of him, as if to check the dampness for himself, one hand slowly came forward, seemed to hover above her left breast as though he would touch her. And while pink started to colour her face, for she wanted his touch, needed his touch, Javier dragged his eyes from her breasts so firmly outlined.

Cally watched, as if in slow motion, the colour that came up under his skin. The way he checked on what he had been going to do. Then his voice was harsh, harsh like she hadn't heard it in a long day.

'For God's sake go and get changed,' he snarled, and turned from her, heading for the bottle of Scotch on the table.

Swiftly Cally went, but not before she had heard him mutter, *'Dios!'* and something, since she had picked up a little Spanish by now, that sounded very like, 'I need a stiff drink.'

CHAPTER NINE

THE easy way he had been with her had gone and never looked like surfacing again, when Cally joined Javier for an early dinner before going on to the Folklore Ballet. For two pins she would have told him to forget about the ballet, but guessing tickets hadn't been easy to obtain, throughout the chilly meal she kept her silence.

He was as courteous as ever he had been, but those little touches, that hand there to turn her this direction or that, as he escorted her through the entrance of the Palacio de las Bellas Artes, were lacking. Sure in her own mind that she had been right to think he was getting tired of squiring her around to places he had most likely been to countless times, she determined then that tomorrow, when he met her from the hospital, she would plead a headache and want nothing more than to return to her room to lie down.

Her spirits were lower than they had ever been, and she had thought it impossible, as they took their seats, for her to enjoy the performance that was about to begin. But from the moment the first dance began, a dance portraying the creation of the Aztec world, through other more colourful dances, *mariarchi* singers and players, until the final curtain came down on a ballet centred round the life in the state of Jalisco, which included the Mexican hat dance, she was enraptured.

Her face couldn't but show her enjoyment, as leaving their seats, unable to thank Javier enough, she told him, her shining eyes showing how wonderful she had thought it all was.

She thought he was going to smile, to revert back to the Javier he had been before, like an idiot, she had gone and stood out in the rain. Oh, why, she fretted, when he did not smile, but offered a polite, 'Bueno,' hadn't she let that spontaneity in her soul stay dead and buried? If she hadn't stood in the rain, had her dress moulded to her, then there would have been nothing to remind Javier of the responsive woman he had once held in his arms—that desire he had once felt now repugnant to him. He would now be treating her as he had all week, in that easy friendly way.

Which, she thought, growing more fed up by the minute as he drove them back to their hotel, was the biggest contradiction she had ever experienced. For she wanted Javier to see her as a woman. She did not want him treating her like—like some younger sister, if he'd had one.

Once in their suite, one look at his face told her the best service she could do him would be to wish him a speedy goodnight and go to her room. But she was stopped by the way he had of constantly surprising her, though it couldn't be because he had noticed there was nothing about her now of the enthralled, shining-eyed creature who had so enjoyed the ballet that he said, before she could get her goodnight out:

'Would—you care for something to eat—a drink of some sort?'

'No, thank you,' she replied politely.

She didn't want his courtesies. She had a feeling she was in for a good howl, and she wanted to be by herself. She took a step nearer her door. But again, that 'goodnight' didn't have a chance to be uttered.

'Your—brother—he is maintaining progress?'

The question seemed to come from him against his

will. And pride soared in Cally then. Obviously he took his duties seriously. He must, she realised, have noticed that she had changed from the enraptured female she had been. Well, the sooner she relieved him of the *duty* of looking after her, the better all round, she thought, feeling bruised to be considered anyone's duty.

'Rolfe,' she said his name deliberately, since apart from that one time, the only name Javier had for him was mud, 'is doing exceptionally well,' adding stiffly, 'It shouldn't be too long now before he's fit enough to leave hospital.'

'I am pleased to hear it.' His tone had gone as stiff as hers. 'You will have no objections, then, if we fly home tomorrow evening?'

Home. She wanted to weep at just that one word, but pride had the tears in check. She might want to go home with him, home to Durango, but from the way he was being, she just had to know it would give him the greatest of pleasure if he could just drop her down and dump her.

'I . . .' she began, biting her lip, knowing what she had to do. 'I think Rolfe can take care of me now.' Oh God, Javier should be cheering at her statement, but instead his brow was looking as black as thunder. She made herself go on. 'I shall not be returning with . . .' It was as far as she got.

In a stride Javier was up to her, had caught hold of her left hand and was angrily bringing it up in front of her face.

'Have you forgotten this?' he demanded. 'Have you forgotten you wear my ring?' he snarled.

'N-no,' she stammered quickly. Then, finding she had more courage than to back down from what looked like being a fight, 'But you've been so—so—well, I thought since you're obviously fed up with—the situation, that this might be the right moment to break . . .'

'I'll let you know when the time is right to break our
engagement.' His voice had quietened to a muted roar.
Then, his tone short, his eyes still blazing, he was telling
her, 'Our engagement was to be for three months,
remember.' And Cally knew if she was riding high on
pride, then his pride must be greater that he intended
keeping on with the farce, as with his jaw thrust
forward, he said, 'When I return to Durango tomorrow,
you come with me—understood?'

She had tried. Even if her heart wasn't in it, she had
tried. And as Cally remembered the way he had been
with her before today, those outings he had taken her
on when he could just as easily have left her to get on
with it, something softened in her. She felt then she
would never be out of his debt—lord knew how much
this luxury suite was going to set him back.

'Understood,' she said quietly. And when that grim
look left him, although her agreement was accepted
without a smile, Cally discovered yet more spontaneity
in her nature. And without knowing quite what she was
doing, she stretched forward and touched her mouth to
his.

Hard hands came instantly to her arms and for a
brief moment she had the uncanniest notion that he was
going to pull her into his arms and carry on from there.
But then she discovered the rapid beat of her heart had
no need to get so excited. For in the next moment he
was pushing her away, grating gruffly:

'What was that for?'

'I'm—grateful. For all you've done—the time you've
taken away from the ranch . . .'

She halted, seeing from his tight-lipped look that if
she had meant to convey her thanks, then it was thanks
he could very well do without.

'When I want your gratitude, I'll ask for it!' was flung
at her. And if she wanted putting in her place, which

she didn't, sarcasm came stinging before he slammed into his bedroom and left her standing. 'Did it escape your notice that I've spent some hours working since we arrived?'

Clearly he had told her his prime reason for coming to Mexico City had not been for her benefit, she saw, standing where he had left her, stunned by the aggression in him. Her gratitude had upset him, she knew that—maybe it went against the grain for him to think he had helped any Shearman, she thought. But she for one would have been sunk if he hadn't taken her with him when he had left Querétaro that day.

Knowing it was going to be hours before she slept, Cally got into her night things and packed all but what she was going to wear tomorrow. She had no choice but to go back to Durango with Javier, but she knew that easy patient way he had been with her was at an end. The outlook for the next two months didn't look to be at all cheerful.

She felt more in control of herself the following morning, and her reserve was out in full force when she joined him in the sitting room. She had heard breakfast arrive two minutes earlier, but wasn't hungry as she offered a business-suited Javier the briefest of good mornings.

Her greeting wasn't answered, which gave her a fair idea of how things were going to be from now on as she poured herself a cup of coffee.

'I have a full day today,' he said instead, 'and may not return until just before we leave for the airport.'

What he was really saying, she guessed, was that if she had been expecting to go on an outing after visiting Rolfe, then she could forget it. She had been going to have a headache anyway, so he needn't have bothered. Without answering, she went to pour him a second cup of coffee; by the look his first one must have gone down scalding hot.

'Don't bother with that,' he stopped her. 'I have an appointment in fifteen minutes.' Cally put down the coffee pot, and still had nothing to say. 'Be packed and ready by seven,' he went on to instruct stiffly.

'Very well,' she obliged, impulse wanting to have her offering to do his packing if he was going to be so very busy. She squashed the impulse—today they were no longer friends, if indeed friends they had ever been.

Her cool reserve had held up from the moment of seeing him. But when, before he went, he reached for his wallet and then coolly went to hand her some notes, her reserve tilted badly sideways, as the words shot from her:

'I don't want your money!'

'You'll need to take a taxi to and from the hospital,' he said, his tone cool, the handful of notes still thrust at her.

'I've money of my own,' she said proudly—but she saw he had the last word, as he dropped the notes down on the table and left.

Determined not to touch a penny—there was enough there for more than half a dozen taxis she saw, with an exasperated thought of, oh, what the hell, she scooped the money up. She had two more months to go, she'd give it back at the first opportunity.

She arrived at the hospital earlier than usual—and initially was very glad that she did. For had she kept to her habit of visiting Rolfe in the early afternoon, she discovered she would not have seen him at all, as when she entered his ward, she saw that not only was he up, but up and dressed.

'Cally!' he exclaimed, a smile breaking. 'I tried to phone you at your hotel a short while back, but there was no reply from your suite.'

There was a question in his voice—a question that was saying that since he obviously hadn't got anywhere asking for her by name, he must then have asked for Javier Zarazua, and learned that she was sharing a suite with him. But to Cally, the explanation was too long and involved then to tell him anything. So she ignored his questioning look, opting to discover what the dickens Rolfe thought he was doing, where on earth did he think he was going. She soon learned he was Acapulco bound.

'But you can't!' she gasped. 'You're not fit—look at you! You . . .'

'Save it, Cally,' he bade her. 'I've heard all you're going to say from the staff here—though for obvious reasons I haven't told them where I'm going.'

'They say it's foolish to leave?' she guessed.

'My mind's made up. I shall be catching a bus in an hour.'

'Bus? But that will take ages. You're not fit . . .'

'I can't get a flight, they're booked solid,' he said, and stubbornly, 'I want to see Yolanda today.'

He was almost swaying on his feet, she thought, but seeing the determination in him, she knew she would be wasting her time trying to talk him out of going, for all she called him idiotically stubborn, and tried.

'I'm going, Cally,' he said, nothing she could say deterring him.

But it was when she learned that the bus ride would take six or seven hours, her affection for him rose up. And there was no way she could let him go alone.

'Then I'm coming with you,' she said, her stubbornness matching his. Her stubbornness dipped. 'That is, if you want me along', she added, only then wondering if he would have tried once more to ring her at the hotel, or if he had intended to disappear without trace yet again, leaving her with no idea when they would ever see each other.

'Of course I want you along,' he said promptly. 'I want Yolanda to meet you. Here,' he said, picking up an envelope and handing it to her, 'I wrote you a note when I couldn't get you at your hotel. I was going to give it to one of the nurses to give you. It tells you where I shall be for the next month—and by the way,' he added, 'I've also included your air fare back to England should you get tired of working for Javier Zarazua and want to go back.'

As he mentioned Javier's name, so the question was back in his voice, but again Cally chose not to hear it. She would have to get back to the hotel and leave Javier a note explaining that she just couldn't allow Rolfe to travel all that way on his own, the state he was in.

'I'll have to dash back to the hotel,' she said, and did away with any explanation by pushing the envelope containing the note and money back at her brother.

'You keep it, love,' he said, refusing to take it, his affection for her showing. 'I promised you your return fare if you made it this far, didn't I?'

'But . . .'

'No buts, little sister,' he grinned, anticipation at seeing his beloved Yolanda back with him. 'You nip back to your hotel and do whatever you have to do, while I phone to get you a seat on the bus. I'll meet you at the coach station in three-quarters of an hour. Can do?'

'Can do,' said Cally knowing she hadn't a second to waste.

In the taxi to the hotel, she composed several different notes to Javier. But it was when she entered her bedroom and saw her case ready packed that the idea came to her to wonder, why bother? Javier didn't care a button what she or Rolfe got up to. And the pain loving him had brought welled up in her—wasn't it far better for her to make the break now? If she went back to Durango with him there would be two long-drawn-out months to suffer. Months when God knew what would happen, with Javier being the cold, unfeeling person he had turned into being with her. Could she take two months of that treatment? And why should she? Hadn't she escaped her father to find a new life?

Cally was in another taxi, her note unwritten, her suitcase on the seat beside her, too late, already regretting she hadn't written a word of explanation to Javier. She knew now that she wouldn't be going back, but she could have written a few words of thanks, she thought—and was angry with herself as the thought came, why? She had tried to show him her gratitude last night and had it thrown back at her—plainly he didn't want her thanks.

The long, long, drive to Acapulco was relieved by the most magnificent scenery Cally had ever thought to see. Forest after mountain forest of trees sped by, trees interspersed with organ cactus springing up tall and straight every now and then.

Cally tried to lose her thoughts in other scenes—a child riding a burro, maize growing everywhere it could be planted, patches of it on cleared sections of mountainside. But when a wayward cow wandered into the road, she was back again in Durango, on Javier's ranch, remembering the many times he had smiled at her, laughed either with or at her—it made no difference. It had her wondering what on earth she was doing going to Acapulco, when where she wanted to be was with him.

And then came the memory of his stern set face as she had seen it that morning, and her fight to be a new Cally Shearman was split in two.

Freedom from the thoughts tearing at her came

unexpectedly from Rolfe who, sitting at her left hand side fast asleep, so she had thought, suddenly poked at the diamond ring on her finger and demanded:

'Hey, what's this?'

Oh, *God*, she had forgotten in her indecision about leaving a note, all about leaving the engagement ring behind. Oh, God in heaven, Javier hadn't believed her when she'd said Rolfe hadn't been interested in any financial gain he might get from marrying Graciela—the diamond was worth a small fortune, he would think . . .

'I think it's about time you told big brother all that's been going on, don't you?' said Rolfe, cutting into her catastrophic thoughts.

'I forgot to give it back,' she said, and could have wept that she was so used to having it on her finger now, she just hadn't given the ring a thought.

'Javier Zarazua,' Rolfe guessed, not seeing it at all strange, she thought, that Javier might have fallen in love with her. Which just showed, she thought, how blind brothers were. 'How long have you been engaged to him?'

'Nearly a month,' she answered absently, in a world of despair.

'Quick work,' commented Rolfe. Which had her sensitive that that there might be any implied criticism of Javier there, and out there in front to defend him.

'How long did it take you to fall in love with Yolanda?' she asked shortly.

'Touché,' he answered easily. Then, seeing more in her answer than she had meant him to see, 'But what are you doing here with me if you love the chap?'

'I—we— We've had—a few words,' she explained, and thought then, that was what it amounted to. Javier was so fed up with her, a few words were about all he could spare.

'It'll all come out in the wash,' was Rolfe's

pronouncement. 'Going to give in first and give him a call tonight?'

'I don't—think so.'

'And you accused me of being stubborn!' he grinned tiredly, and promptly went back to sleep.

The dark-haired girl who met them off the bus in the steaming heat of Acapulco was not as beautiful as from Rolfe's description Cally had imagined her to be. But what she lacked in beauty, she made up for by being just the way she was. And before long Cally could see what it was about her that had Rolfe sunk without trace.

The warmth in Yolanda's smile, the tenderness there as she exclaimed over Rolfe's still bruised face, the way the two of them clung together, told Cally that this was a love match. If only Javier . . .

She stopped her thoughts right there. Javier would never love her. Right at this moment he was most likely hating just the very thought of her. Oh, *why* hadn't she thought to leave that ring behind?

For two days Cally stuck it out in Acapulco. Kitted out in a swimsuit, she sampled as other tourists did the magnificent rolling surf that stormed up to the shoreline, snatched you up and took you back with them, then just as you were getting panicky, threw you back on to the shoreline again, and left you with grains of coarse sand on the inside of your swimsuit.

Conscious that Rolfe and Yolanda didn't need a third person to complete their happiness at being together again, she kept out of their way as much as possible. One morning she took a trip in a glass-bottomed boat, and knew exactly why, when the engine was stopped some half hour out and one of the crew dived overboard and appeared beneath the glass panelling, exactly why she couldn't get excited about it. There was no Javier with her.

Acapulco bay was a superb scene of rocks and hills,

which any other time she was sure she would have found stunning. But Javier ate into her every thought. Memory was there of the time he had revealed his opinion of her as a female who had come to Mexico after the 'pickings' had changed. The knowledge was with her that he would now be kicking himself for having been so deceived by her.

She had to get that ring back to him, of course. But how? Standing shaded by an almond tree, Cally pondered on trusting the valuable item to the mail. It would make only a small parcel—look well if it got lost.

That night when both Yolanda and Rolfe insisted she went with them to La Quebrada to see the high-divers, Cally said she thought she would have an early night.

'You had an early night last night,' Rolfe objected. And playfully, 'That much sleep ain't healthy, kid!' Then, promptly dropping his air of fun, he enquired, 'Have you made that phone call yet?'

'So I'll come with you to see the high-divers,' she countered, aware now that since nothing was secret between her brother and Yolanda, that he had told her she was engaged to Javier, and that they had had a row.

Cally stood in awe as the fit young diver scaled up the rocks to take his place on the diving platform. To her mind that precarious ascent looked as dangerous as the dive into the lapping waters below. She had heard the divers counted the waves in before, the number right, they took off. And with Javier for the rare occasion not on her mind, she closed her eyes in fear for the diver's life when he took off. The applause that broke out had her peering to look into the water. In her view the clapping was premature. Far better, she thought, for everyone to wait until the diver reappeared before they saluted his bravery. Her fear for his safety evaporated when she saw him appear where she had not been looking, so perhaps the rest of the audience had

seen him sooner, she thought, and promptly forgot him
as Javier took over her thoughts again.

It was when they were on their way back to their
hotel in the beetle Volkswagen taxi that the idea came
to her to ask Rolfe to return the ring to Javier for her.
The enervating heat of Acapulco seemed to suit him, or
maybe it was just from the tonic of seeing Yolanda
again, that he was improving daily. He could fly to
Durango, she thought; that wouldn't be anywhere near
as exhausting as that bus ride here had been.

'Rolfe,' she said, when the taxi had been paid off and
they walked into their hotel. She had his attention, saw
he was looking at her. And then as she saw there was
still a faint discolouration on his face, denoting all he
had been through, her intention to get something
constructive done about that ring rather than spend
another sleepless night in stewing over it vanished.
'Nothing,' she said lamely.

'Ring him,' he advised, and they all got into the lift.

Having arranged to meet Yolanda and Rolfe by the
hotel swimming pool next morning, Cally was first
there and anxious to see her brother.

Her indecision was at an end. There was only one
thing she could do, and she was amazed at herself that
she hadn't realised it before. It would take courage, she
knew that. But she hadn't turned her back on her old
life only to have that moral cowardice in being unable
to stand up to her father follow her.

Rolfe saw, as soon as he looked into her determined
face, that her hours of agonising were over. 'You're
going to ring him,' he stated as soon as he had got
Yolanda comfortably settled on a lounger.

'I've decided to go and see him,' Cally said quietly—
and discovered then what a dear brother she had.

'You'll want the first flight out, by the look of you,'
he said seriously. Then turning to Yolanda he told her

he was going with Cally to book an air ticket, and would soon be back.

That Rolfe had shed his wild ways, his love for Yolanda having matured an air of responsibility in him, was much in evidence from the way he wouldn't let Cally pay for her air ticket, even though she protested she still had the other money he had given her.

'You won't need it for your ticket to England,' he said confidently, causing her to realise that was exactly what it was going to be spent on, 'so buy yourself a wedding present with it from Yolanda and me.'

Knowing there would be too many complications if she told him there wasn't the remotest likelihood of there being any wedding, Cally reached up and kissed him.

Both he and Yolanda went with her to the airport, Yolanda being very sweet and giving her the same hug her brother had the minute before given her.

'I know you're averse to phoning a chap,' said Rolfe, tongue in cheek, 'but give me a ring within the next three and a half weeks, we'll be moving on after that.'

Even without having any idea what Javier had told Teresa and Arturo when he had gone back to the homestead without her, Cally was sure, as her plane landed in Durango, that he wouldn't want her anywhere near his home.

Accordingly, she booked into a modest hotel, realised it was getting late, and was on edge to get it all over and done with. Common sense told her it would be better to wait until the morning, as Javier could have gone out to dinner.

At nine that might, however she picked up the phone and asked for his number. If he was out, she had tried. If he was at home, then though she knew she was in for a rough time, at least she would be hearing the sound of that voice she felt starved for.

The waiting seemed endless as nerves got to her—
nerves that very nearly had her putting down the
receiver. Then she heard his voice, Javier's voice
speaking in his native Mexican, and she was hanging on
to the phone as though glued to it, hearing the
impatience in his voice that nobody was answering him.
Impatience she knew would very soon turn into anger
and be fully directed at her.

'J-Javier,' she choked, and heard the terrible long-
drawn-out silence, before at long last, her voice
recognised, his voice came again, in English this time,
chilly, so very level she just had to know he was
striving for control, control not to roar at her as she
deserved.

'Cally?—Cally, is that you?' he asked, just as though
he couldn't believe it. Couldn't believe after she had
walked off with that very valuable diamond, she could
have the audacity to phone him.

CHAPTER TEN

'Y-YES—it's me,' Cally whispered, wiping her eyes with the back of her hand. And as all thought-out phrases eluded her, she said, inanely she afterwards thought, 'I—went to Ac—Acapulco.'

'What the——' he rapped, his even way of speaking soon departing, so that Cally, having anticipated his anger, was unable to take it and was butting in:

'I went with Rolfe . . .'

'I *know* that,' he came back savagely, causing her to know he must have been so mad to find her gone, his diamond gone with her, yet his first reaction had been to race to the hospital. But he was giving her no time to think further. Though it did seem he was doing his best to get himself under control.

'Where in Acapulco?' he asked, his voice more even. 'Which hotel are you in?'

'I'm not in—Acapulco,' she revealed—and realised his temper hadn't stayed controlled for more than a few seconds, as he roared in her ears:

'Then where the *hell* are you?'

Anything to pacify him, Cally quickly gave him the name of her hotel, adding, 'It's here. Here in Durango.'

'You're in Durango!' He sounded shattered, she thought, that she'd got the nerve to come this close.

'I forgot I was wearing your ring when I went,' she explained in a rush—and knew then his anger was more than he could contain, when the words came whirling along the line, the moment before the phone was slammed down:

170

'It strikes me you conveniently forgot a lot of other
ngs as well!'

Numbed, Cally stared at the phone in her hand,
fore her phone too went back on its rest. She made
 attempt to get undressed and into bed, but began
cing the room, her thoughts too many, too agonised,
 be borne by lying still.

Half an hour later, she had calmed somewhat, but
is still too churned up to find rest. Knowing she
uld never have the nerve to ring Javier again, not
night anyway, she hoped when he had cooled down,
 might ring her, maybe tell her to leave the ring with
 hotel management for him to collect. But when
other half an hour had gone by, and not one peep
d been heard from the phone, Cally knew he
uldn't be ringing.

He would phone tomorrow, she thought, trying to
ok at the situation logically. Though since she would
ve to wait for his call, she had better hang on to
ke her arrangements to get back to England.

A sudden peremptory knocking on her door had her
iving her thoughts and going to answer it. And as her
ce paled, Javier being the last person she expected to
 standing there, his eyes looking like blue chips of
, he calmly pushed the door wide, and just as calmly
 walked into her room.

'Good,' he said, his eyes going over her. 'I see you
en't in bed yet. Get your things together.'

'My—things?' she echoed, uncomprehendingly, just
 sight of him in navy slacks and sweater sending her
ught patterns haywire, making her unable to make
y sense whatsoever of what he was saying.

'You're checking out,' he said, his tone brooking no
gument. 'Correction,' he amended. 'You've just
ecked out—I've settled your bill.'

'But—but where are . . .' you taking me, she would

have added, but was stopped by the slight thawing that
came over him, as intently he looked into her face.

'You look tired,' he commented briefly. Then he
was taking charge by hefting her case up from the floor,
was opening it, and while she stood by floundering, he
was opening wardrobes, going to the bathroom and
coming back stuffing her toothbrush inside her toilet
bag, and had in fact packed the few things she had
unpacked before she had fully comprehended what was
going on.

And then it was self-preservation pure and simple
that had her saying stiffly. 'I'm not going anywhere
with you, Javier. I—only came back to give you this.'
Swiftly she drew the beautiful diamond from her finger
and held it out to him.

But she did not feel the loss of it for very long. Barely
was it off her finger, before Javier had taken hold of the
ring and her left hand, and in no time he had pushed
the ring back home.

'You agreed to be engaged to me for three months,
señorita,' he barked at her. 'No one breaks their word
to me, and that includes you!' And while she was
gasping that he couldn't really mean what he was
saying, he was adding toughly, 'Either you walk or I
carry you out of here—make up your mind.'

Cally sat stiffly beside him in his car, as with his face
still thunderous, Javier drove furiously in the night. She
had had no alternative but to come with him, that
reserve in her unable to take the chance that he
wouldn't carry out his threat and stride through the
hotel foyer in front of everyone with her kicking and
screaming over his shoulder.

He knew that too, damn him, she thought, growing
mutinous. He knew about that something in her that
would cringe against being made a show of in public.

All the way in that silent drive to the homestead, she

utinied against his high-handed way with her. So he
as anxious not to lose face in the community. And
viously he hadn't told anyone that their engagement
as off. Though surely he could have invented some-
ing to the effect she'd had to return to England
a hurry, that her father was ill—anything.

Cally knew full well what lay at the bottom of her
jection to being made to return to the homestead.
e was afraid. Afraid if Javier insisted she stay for
other two months, not only would it be so much
rse when the time came for her to leave, but that
ce she loved him so very much, he might in those two
onths discover just how things were with her—her
ide would never stand that.

Mutiny deserted her soul from the first sight she had
the dear familiar homestead. She didn't know how
e kept back tears when Javier pulled up at the front
trance, but she managed to keep her face straight as
e got out of the car and went inside with him.

'I'll take your case to your room, then unless you
quire any refreshment, I suggest you go straight to
d.'

'I want nothing,' she said quietly, as her eyes went
vingly round the white walls of the hall. And she
dn't get a second chance to refuse as, taking her at her
rd, Javier went up the stairs and had the door of her
droom open, her suitcase deposited, when she joined
m.

She would have gone by him without a word. She did
t want that his hand should come out to touch her, to
aken her as she would have stepped by him. She did
t want that, his aim achieved in having brought her
ck, his tough aggression should have left him, as he
id:

'Goodnight, Cally. Sleep well.'

'Goodnight,' she said abruptly, and not wanting to

look at him, did just that, looked up, her eyes revealing unhappy thoughts as they looked into his.

She felt his hand, warm, relenting, come to the side of her face. 'Do not take it so hard, sweet Cally,' he said softly, and he had her rooted, as gently he kissed her, then went quickly from the room.

Oh, why did he have to kiss her? she groaned, tears spilling down her face. Here was she trying with all she had to be cool, remote, and he had to go and do that.

She got undressed and into her night things, tears she could do nothing about falling like rain down her cheeks, letting her know just how much she had changed from the girl she had once been. While living with her father she had never cried—never cried, she realised, simply because she hadn't been living. Now, out of that sterile vacuum, she was feeling, hurting, just like other people hurt, and it was painful when she had known none of the pain of loving before. And still her tears fell.

When an irritating tickle attacked her throat, Cally began to feel her despair was absolute. For ages now she had been without that exhausting cough. To have it return now, brought on by tiredness, obviously, since she couldn't remember the last time she'd had a good night's sleep, was untenable.

Racked by a fit of coughing, she knew some warm lemonade would do the trick. But memory of that other time she had crept downstairs in the middle of the night was with her, and nothing would have had her repeating the exercise.

Never had Cally felt more miserable in her life as she sat in her thin cotton dressing gown on the edge of the bed, wiping away tears that were as much from the hurt and sadness in her as from the coughing attack, that now, thank goodness, seemed to be letting up. Brushing her hair from her eyes, she caught sight of the sparkling nond—and the floodgates opened again.

[H]ow long Javier had stood there watching her, she
 no idea. Probably only a second, she thought, for
 had been so wrapped up in trying to calm herself
 her feelings, she had not so much as heard the door
[ope]n. She had been totally unaware of his physical
[pre]sence, till he moved and she saw him. She gasped,
 coughed again as, still in shirt and slacks, his sweater
[rem]oved as if he had been in the process of undressing
[whe]n he had heard her coughing, he came forward and
[mad]e her drink from the warm glass in his hand.

['Y]ou lost that cough within a very short time of
[com]ing to my home,' he said quietly. And while
[mir]aculously her throat was eased, 'It would seem,
[wou]ld it not, that you are not so well suited to the
[clim]ate of Acapulco as you are to Durango.'

[S]ally wished her tears could be as easily checked as
 lemonade had checked her coughing, could have
[wish]ed Javier wasn't being nice to her; it was no help at
 [all] in the battle she was having to stop crying. She
[wan]ted him to go, yet he didn't appear to be in any
[hur]ry to return to his room now that her coughing had
[eas]ed. And she was oh, so terribly afraid that with that
[shar]p discernment he had, he would soon see that now
 [she] was no longer coughing, there was no reason why
 [her] eyes should still be watering.

['I'll] be all right now,' she said, turning her face away.
['Th]ank . . .'

[H]is hand came beneath her chin, and although she
[trie]d to pull away, those firm fingers were determined,
[it se]emed, to have her look at him.

[S]he raised misty eyes to his, but had no chance to
[iden]tify what expression he wore. Though since his
[han]d was firmly gentle on her chin, she hoped—didn't
[car]e, that he was still being nice to her, and knew
[hers]elf confused when, letting go her chin, he came and

sat on the edge of the bed beside her.

'Tears, Cally?' he queried, a roughness there tha
wasn't hostile, but which she couldn't pin down a
having heard quite that quality in him before. 'Are you s
unhappy to be back in my home that it makes you cry?

Immediately she wanted to disabuse him of that idea
And knew she would be wise to exercise caution—an
she had two months to go yet.

'I—it isn't—that,' she replied slowly, finding a hank
in her dressing gown pocket and doing the best sh
could to make her face more presentable, fortun
favouring her in that her unhappy tears appeared t
have dried.

'What, then?' he asked quietly, and she was nowher
near to finding an answer.

'It doesn't matter,' she tried, and wasn't allowed t
get away with it.

'I think it does.'

Overwhelmingly aware of his nearness, Cally wa
sitting next to the bed end, with no possibility of edgin
away. She felt Javier take her right hand, and that wa
no help either, as he soothed his thumb over the back o
it.

'I know you do not cry easily Cally,' he sai
thoughtfully. 'The times I have seen you in tears hav
been warranted, a natural release from some emotiona
anguish . . .'

'Don't!'

The word came from her quickly, in panic that h
was getting too close. She thought then that that on
word 'Don't' had revealed too much. But when Javie
questioned the word, she knew only relief that he hadn'
associated her emotional anguish as having anything t
do with him—her feelings for him.

'Don't?' She heard a lighter note enter his voice then
as, waiving the answer to his question, he said, 'Do no

be afraid of your emotions, *niña*. Do not repress them. I would far rather you admitted that you are feeling unhappy at parting from the brother you have so recently been reunited with than to think you are unhappy that I have brought you back home.'

Brought you back home, she thought dreamily. How naturally he had said that! It had sounded just as though he thought the homestead her home, and nowhere else. Abruptly she pulled herself together. Whatever it had sounded like, Javier hadn't meant it to sound that way. It was just his way of speaking. English was not his first language, she had to remind herself, although he was as at home in her language as his own.

'Am I right—is it because you have parted from Rolfe that you are so sad?' he pressed, when she had nothing to say.

'I—shall miss him,' she prevaricated.

'But you will see him again.'

She could hear the smile in him as he tried to cheer her up. And since, sunk to the depths before he had entered her room, she couldn't stay down, not while he was with her, not until he had gone could she allow unhappy thoughts entry, Cally made a determined effort to get on top.

'Of course I shall,' she said brightly. And when she dared to turn her head to offer what she could in the way of a smile, she saw Javier was smiling too, and was glad she had made the effort.

'If it is your wish,' he said, slowly then, 'I have no objection if you invite him here.'

Astonishment faded her smile. 'You'd have him *here*!'

'If it is your wish.'

'But . . .'

Taken out of her stride, she could only stare at him. And she felt the weakness of tears again that Javier, who must surely hate Rolfe for what he had done to his

family, should because his pride wouldn't allow that she
should be unhappy in his home, fretting as she had let
him believe, that she had said goodbye to Rolfe, turn
his back on his hate so she should find the next two
months more bearable.

'I couldn't do that to you, Javier,' she said quietly.

'Couldn't do what?'

'Allow you to sink one pride for another.'

Whether he caught on to what she was really saying,
he gave no clue. But he had alarm speeding through her
when quietly, he said:

'Love conquers all pride.'

Had he guessed she had little pride where he was
concerned? She had lost her pride when she had cried
all over him. As recently as a few minutes ago he had
seen her in tears. With rapid haste she got him away
from the subject of love.

'I doubt if I shall see Rolfe again before I go to
England,' she said hurriedly, and words were spilling
from her in her agitation as she saw Javier's sharp
interest. Pray God it was interest in what she had just
said. 'Yolanda and Rolfe will stay in Acapulco for a
few weeks, and then will be moving on. He'll write to
me in England, of course—though I haven't made any
arrangements about that.' She had only just remembered
she didn't have a home in England to go to. 'He'll have
to write care of a post office or something until I get
settled,' she heard herself babbling on.

'You have no home with your father?'

Cally still felt agitated. The sudden hardness she
heard in Javier did not help her agitation, although she
could see no reason for him to suddenly get up tight.

'I told you,' she reminded, managing to keep the
flurry inside her from showing, 'he's remarrying—the
house was up for sale when I left.'

'You also said there was no place for you in his

home,' he said tersely, proving she had no need to remind him of anything. 'Did you mean there was no room in the new accommodation?'

'I—don't want to go there,' she hedged—and knew when Javier said, what he *shatteringly* did say next, that he had the answer to his question—that her father did not want her living with him.

'You could stay here,' he offered coolly. 'You could make your home here if you wish.'

Sure she couldn't be hearing right, she stared at him again, only just managing to stop her mouth from gaping.

'You mean——' she began, her all-over-the-place thoughts sorting themselves out to what he really meant, 'you mean, stay in Mexico—stay in Durango?'

'I mean,' he said, that cool way still with him, 'you could stay on here—here in my home.'

'No!' Her reply was sharp and instant. It had his brows coming together in a dark frown. But for Cally there was no other answer. She had no idea yet how she was going to get through the next two months. She just did not dare let herself think of staying longer. To see him every day, to dine with him, to work with him— she shut her thoughts off sharply. 'No,' she said again, and had to mean it.

'It is not as I thought, then,' Javier challenged toughly. 'It *is* because you are unhappy here that you are weeping.'

'No, no, *no!*' she cried, wanting to get up and walk away from him, but finding she was somehow wedged now between him and the bedpost. She knew she had to be calm, knew she was doing herself no favours by getting excited. She took a deep breath, aware from his grim expression that he wasn't believing her, and said as evenly as she could, 'My place is in England. I—I love your country—but in two months' time, I shall return to England.'

He wasn't liking what she was saying, she could tell that. Even her admitting she loved his country, as she did, had not lightened his dark look. And suddenly he seemed as fed up with her as he had been back in that hotel in Mexico City.

'Then go, damn you!' he said harshly. 'I shall do nothing to stop you. As soon as our arrangement is terminated,' so, fed up or not, his pride was keeping her to that, 'I personally will purchase your air ticket.'

That hurt. It turned a knife in her, that in seconds he could be so careless of her that he could change from a man who had offered her a roof, to a man who couldn't wait for the day he could get rid of her. And her own pride surfaced. There wasn't a tear about her, when proudly she lifted her head and loftily told him:

'You can keep your money, Javier Zarazua Guerrero! I can pay my own air fare.'

'You can . . .? Where did you get it?' he rapped. 'Who gave it to you?'

'Rolfe. My brother, if you must know,' she said hotly, not backing down, although his aggression was growing mighty.

Then all at once she was aware of a tension that had come to him, a tension that communicated itself to her, a tension that started to bite into her. Something had struck him, she knew it—knew it, without knowing what it was. Silence stretched tautly as she mentally went back over what she had said, but could see nothing there that should have him as tense as a trap waiting to go off.

Then he was breaking the silence, and Cally was very nearly going under with what he had seen that she had so sublimely not seen.

'You have your air fare, yet you returned to Durango? The place you appear most anxious to be

away from?' His tone was cool, but there was
something else there too—a suggestion there that had
her wary, that he was more than interested in her
answer.

'I've—told you why I came back.' He'd got to believe
it, even if only now was she realising she had been lying
to herself. 'I forgot to return your ring. I—I told you
that.' And, belabouring the point in her need to get him
to believe her, 'That ring was the—the only reason
I . . .'

'Was it, Cally?'

Oh, God, this was dreadful. She'd die of embarrassment if he didn't let go, if he discovered. 'Good
heavens, Javier,' she shrugged, her voice going just a
touch higher in her controlled panic, 'what other reason
could there be?' And before he could get started, she
was in there quickly with, 'I really think you should go.
Look at the time—we'll both be fit for nothing in the
morning.'

'You're getting panicky, *chica*,' he observed softly.
And, doing nothing to ease that panic, 'Why, Cally?
What is it that frightens you?'

'Nothing. Nothing frightens me. I j-just want you to
go, so I c-can get to my bed.' She licked dry lips, then
hurriedly reminded him, 'You said yourself I looked
tired.'

She held herself stiffly when that comment brought
his eyes to study her face. Then, unable to bear his
scrutiny, afraid what might be revealed there, uncaring
now that it might be ungainly, she pushed her way out
from between him and the bedpost, and went to stand
the other side of a carved rounded chair in the room.

'Tired you may be,' said Javier, getting to his feet, his
hands going casually into his trousers pockets, 'but I
doubt you will find sleep in the agitated state you are
in.'

'I'm unlikely to find sleep until you've gone either, am I?' she fired, and could have groaned out loud that she had as good as admitted that she was indeed agitated.

'Then the remedy to both problems seems to be in your hands,' he said suavely. 'All you have to do is tell me why, when you could have used half a dozen methods to get that ring back to me, you came in person—then I will leave you.'

'I—I made a bargain with you to stay for two months,' Cally said desperately.

'But you were ready to renege on that bargain when I came to Durango to get you,' he reminded her.

'I—I,' she said helplessly, too late realising she had spoken without thinking first. 'Well, I—was having second thoughts,' she rallied. 'You were—sounded . . .' she was struggling, 'back in Mexico City—that—at the end, you seemed as if you didn't want me around. I remembered that when I got to Durango—I—er—thought then that . . .'

'You're a hopeless liar, Cally Shearman—do you know that?'

And it was then that Cally blew it. She just couldn't take any more. And all her efforts to keep him from knowing the truth went up in spirited flames, as she blazed, 'Damn you Javier, I love you! Now call me a liar!'

The silence in the room was deafening. Whatever he had been expecting, it couldn't have been that, she thought, wanting the ground to open up and swallow her as she saw him stand as though rooted. As she saw the way his face lost some of its colour.

Unable to bear that astounded look on his face, she swiftly presented him with her back, choking back tears as she grabbed at what pride she had left, and told him formally:

'Please go, *señor*. You wanted retribution for what my brother did to your family—I think one unrequited love is fair exchange for another.' She heard him move, and had one last thing to say before he closed the door behind him. 'Tomorrow I shall return to England.'

The next sound she had been expecting to hear, as with her back erect she stood, was the door handle turning. So the shock that rioted in her when two firm hands came to her arms and he turned her to face him had her startled and instinctively backing, trying to be free.

But Javier, it appeared, had no intention of letting her go. And he had a few words of his own to surprise her with—even if, since she would not raise her head and look at him, they had to be addressed to the top of her blonde waves.

'And what, little Cally mine,' he said softly, apparently over the shock she had seen in his face, which was more than she could say for herself, unable to believe as she was that she had actually said what she had, 'what would you have me do about our engagement?'

'Can't—can't you think up some story?' she mumbled. 'I know losing face worries you, b-but I'll go along with anything you . . .'

'Loss of face? No, *querida* Cally, what people say of me is not important to me,' was the first surprise he had for her.

'But——' she protested, still not able to look at him, doubting she ever would again, 'that's why we got engaged, wasn't it?'

'We became engaged to save *your* face in the light of Teresa's—naughty thoughts,' he told her lightly, and seemed suddenly to be having a hard time holding down some irrepressible good humour.

It was all right for him, she thought unhappily, and

she lost no time to tell him shortly, 'Well, you certainly wanted tit-for-tat with my family. That was the only reason you brought me here in the first place, to . . .'

'How you love to jump to conclusions,' he observed, when she knew very well all her conclusions had been accurate. 'I needed a reason for bringing you with me, certainly.' She heard a smile enter his voice. 'I *had* to bring you back with me, Cally. There was no way I could leave Querétaro without you.'

Because she was as near broke as dammit, she thought, puzzlement entering, since the way he had been then, he should have been delighted at the prospect of leaving her stranded. Chivalry? she wondered. If it wasn't to get even by making her soil her hands he had thought had never so much as touched a duster—was it chivalry in his soul that had him not wanting to leave her stranded?

'I could have gone to the British Consulate,' she said stiffly. 'Once I told them I was short of funds . . .'

'You being short of funds, though broke is what I would have called it,' he told her, 'was the biggest stroke of good fortune for me.'

'Well, I'm glad about that,' she snapped, and made a futile attempt to get free of his hands. Then, her puzzlement not being denied, she found she was having to ask, 'Why?'

'You don't know?' Javier queried softly. She shook her head. That teasing had not left him, his soft tones were treacherously threatening to melt her. 'You have no idea?' he asked.

Cally thought, and could come up with nothing. Though she thought she might have been able to associate it with something had she not been all haywire from her blurted out confession of love for him, had he not been in her room—had he not been there holding her, talking softly to her.

'None,' she said. 'None at all.' And suddenly she was
ipping on to him, her head jerked up, disbelief filling
r eyes, when tenderly he said:

'Have you had so little loving in your life, my Cally,
at you cannot see—I care for you?'

'You—care—for *me*!'

His eyes were telling her he did. It was there in the
nder smile for her that curved his lips. But she still
sn't believing it.

'Why else should I rejoice to see the meagre contents
your wallet?' he said softly, his eyes holding hers so
e couldn't look away.

'You wanted me broke?'

'I wanted you in my home. Your being virtually
nniless gave me a foothold. Yes, my love, I wanted
u broke.'

'But ...' Floundering as she had never floundered
fore, Cally was arguing, 'But you didn't even like me
en.'

'I liked myself even less,' he said, one hand leaving its
ld on her arm to smooth her hair back from her face.
was hating myself for the power you had over me
m the first moment I held you in my arms.'

'When I fainted,' she remembered.

'I thought it was just tiredness then. I had no idea of
e remains of that virus in you that was taking such a
ie to depart,' he said, his face shadowing as if he
ted himself for putting her to work straight away.
at look melted some of the disbelief in her, and as
r heart began to thunder a cacophony she felt sure
uld make itself heard, the shadows left him, and he
s saying, 'I caught you in my arms—and knew you
re my life.'

'Oh, Javier!' she said tremulously, and found two
ong arms around her.

'Oh, Cally,' was his reply, as making no attempt to

kiss her, he held her to him, and looked deep into her eyes, deep into her very soul. 'I wanted you broke, my angel,' he breathed, 'needed that foothold, any foothold, that meant I didn't have to let you go.'

'You didn't want me to—leave Mexico?'

'I never want you to leave Mexico, not unless I come with you.'

Cally laid her head against his chest, peace coming over her. As yet it was all too incredible, she was afraid to even pinch herself in case she should wake up and find all this was a dream.

For minutes Javier held her to his heart, content just to have her there, letting her see how it had been with him, by softly stroking her hair and telling her how so much had he wanted her with him, that even before he had called to collect her at her hotel in Querétaro, he had telephoned Teresa telling her to prepare a guest room, in the profound hope that he could think of some way of getting her to go with him.

'Honestly?' said Cally, raising her head to stare at him in wonder.

'Honestly, my little disbeliever,' he said, and his arms tightening, threatening to crack her ribs. '*Dios,* how I love you, my beautiful Cally!'

His words had her gripping on to him in return. And it was then that their lips met, her arms going round him as passion ruled him, and he kissed her throat, her ears, her eyes, then just looked at her—and looked at her, and had her crying helplessly:

'Oh, Javier, I love you so—I thought my heart would break!'

Spanish was his language then as, with an exultant roar, he picked her up in his arms and carried her to the bed. Endearments, the meaning she had no knowledge of, were showered down on her, and she received them like refreshing rain after a dry parched summer. And he

as kissing her, caressing her, unable to get close
ough to his love, his life, as he pressed against her,
nding her mindless of all thought save that he was her
fe too, and that she loved him.

'*Te quiero. Te amo,*' he breathed, a caressing hand
nfastening her robe, that hand moving to capture her
reast.

Cally kissed him and had no thought of holding back
hile his hands were on her, gentle, unhurried, pacing
er urgency for him. '*Te amo?*' she asked huskily.

'It means, I love you,' he whispered, and smiled into
er eyes when she recalled:

'You said that—that first week I was here—that day
the overseer's house.'

'Did I not say I knew from the first you were my
fe?' he asked tenderly.

'Oh, Javier,' she whispered again, 'I wish I'd known
en.'

'I don't think you would have appreciated it then, my
eart,' he smiled. 'Physically I had discovered we were
ne, but I don't think, in your reserved little soul, you
ere in love with me then?'

'Perhaps not,' she admitted. 'Though I don't think
s in me to do—er—do this sort of thing with any
an—so I think something must have been happening
my . . .' she broke off to give a laugh of pure delight,
eserved little soul, even then.' And, more seriously, as
e recalled, 'I discovered I loved you when we checked
to our hotel in Mexico City—that second time I cried
over you.'

Javier would have kissed her then, but his love was so
ew to her, Cally's small frown of puzzlement had him
tting aside his own desires, and anxious to take that
own from her.

'What is it, *mi amor*? Tell me. Nothing must hurt or
set you ever again.'

'If you love me, why were you so cold to me at the end of our stay in Mexico City?'

'Love you? I adore you, my little sweetheart,' he breathed, and queried, 'But cold?' before he conceded, 'Maybe I appeared so, but it was not the way I was feeling inside. Inside there had been a furnace stoking up all week. It was a mistake to have you in that suite so close to me—but,' he confessed, 'it was where I wanted you to be. I thought I could handle it, thought . . .' He broke off to plant a tiny kiss on her mouth. 'I was doing quite well, I thought. And then one day you forgot the strictures instilled in you from childhood and went dancing out in the rain.' Undying devotion was in his eyes when, his voice thickened, he said, 'Desire for your body is a natural part of my loving for you—do you mind?'

'Not a bit,' she came back swiftly, and went pink as the promptitude of her reply had him raising a delighted eyebrow. Cally's inherent shyness had her reminding him fast about Mexico City. 'You were saying?' she queried, and heard his unrestrained laugh.

'I was saying, my forward young madam,' he said, and then went on, deadly serious, 'that seeing you that day, with little left to the imagination in that wet dress you had on, I came near to taking you right there and then. The only way I could counteract it, since I wanted not just your body but you as well, was to be the opposite of what I was feeling.' He kissed her again, then said, 'I never wanted to hurt you, my love.'

Cally kissed him to show if he had hurt her, then it didn't matter, his love was all that mattered. Then she discovered that if she had been hurt, he had been very nearly demented when he had returned to the hotel the day she had gone to Acapulco.

'I couldn't believe it,' he said, a trace of the agony he had been through showing in his eyes. 'I expected you

be there waiting for me, and still didn't believe you
uld have gone even when I checked your room and
.w that neither your clothes nor your case were there.'

'Forgive me?' she asked gently, wanting to take that
ok away. And she smiled.

And Javier smiled back. 'I'll forgive you anything
oviding you love me,' he said. And at her assurance
.at the word love didn't begin to convey the feeling in
:r heart she had for him, he pressed his lips to hers,
.d all was silent for many beautiful minutes.

A tap on the door had him unhurriedly taking one
m from around her to cover her with her robe, then
rning to face the door. And Cally's face was already a
arm pink when the door opened, and she saw Teresa
anding there. Only this time she saw there was a smile
. Teresa's face as she looked over to the bed to the
/o of them.

There was a quick exchange of Spanish between
.vier and Teresa, and then, leaving the bedroom door
ide, Teresa had bidden her, *'Buenas noches, señorita,'*
.d had departed.

'There are times when I think seriously of parting
.th Teresa's services,' said Javier, sitting up and taking
ally with him.

'No!' said Cally promptly.

'You like her?'

'Yes, yes, I do,' she said equally promptly.

'In that case, I shall let her stay,' he grinned, and she
.ew then he hadn't been seriously contemplating
tting rid of Teresa. 'She said she heard you coughing
rlier, and saw your light on when she came to listen at
.ur door if you were settled.'

'The darling!' said Cally affectionately.

'That wasn't what I just called her, but since she was
iiling when she removed herself, I doubt she has
ken it to heart.'

He then took hold of her left hand, and raising it to his lips, tenderly he kissed the place where she wore his ring. And still holding on to her hand, his fingers on that seal that said she was promised to him, he said regretfully:

'I will leave you now, Cally *mi vida*, but only if you will promise to wake early—I shall be impatient to see you.'

'You're not working tomorrow?'

'I hope to have a lot to arrange,' he said. And his eyes showed his love for her. 'With this ring feeling so comfortable on your finger you forgot to return it— May I soon put its comfortable companion there behind it?'

Cally thought it the most beautiful of marriage proposals. And love was shining from her eyes too, as she whispered, 'Soon—yes—soon, please, Javier!'

Harlequin® Plus
A WORD ABOUT THE AUTHOR

sica Steele was born in Leamington, in England's
dlands, next to the last in a close-knit family of seven
ldren. As a child and young woman, she waged a long
ttle with illness — but she emerged with a strong spirit
it stands her in good stead still.

At a time when things seemed most bleak in her life,
sica had the good fortune to meet a man who was to
come her second husband, Peter. Two years after their
rriage, Jessica sat down to try her hand at writing
nething other than the poetry she had composed for
own satisfaction. Her first attempt at a love story was
ected, and it was then that she began to understand
y it was that her mother had often called her a
bborn child. She was to write another seven stories
ore she was sent the acceptance letter she was waiting
. Her first book was *Spring Girl* (Harlequin Romance
289), published in 1979.

Throughout it all, her husband was a source of
stant encouragement, and when Jessica was able to
ign her civil-service job to concentrate on her writing
eer, it was a credit to the perseverance of them both!